BEDEVILED

BEDEVILED

a novella

PAT MATSUEDA

Mānoa Books
HONOLULU

El León Literary Arts
BERKELEY

2017

Part of "Waif" originally appeared in *Eleven Eleven*, the literary journal of the California College of the Arts.

First edition published 2016 by

Mānoa Books
an imprint of Mānoa Foundation, of Honolulu, Hawai'i
manoafoundation.org

El León Literary Arts, of Berkeley, California
elleonliteraryarts.org

Second edition published 2017 by
Mānoa Books   El León Literary Arts
and distributed by Lulu.com

ISBN 978-0-9799504-1-4
Printed in the United States of America

Designed by Peak Services (peakserviceshawaii.com) and composed in Brioso Pro (created by Robert Slimbach) and Carlin Script (created by Hans-Jürgen Ellenberger). Fleurons are from Fleurons Rogers (created by Bruce Rogers).

contents

part i

Man's devil is man himself.

INTIZAR HUSAIN

Come, evil one, that I may kiss you.

FIRĀQ GŌRAKPŪRĪ

over the pali

Sitting in a dark bedroom of his home in Kāneʻohe, Ted Koga stared at the black-and-silver laptop. Several feet away slept his two sons. He had turned the screen away from them so they wouldn't wake, but he was ready to close the browser in an instant. The boys were so sensitive that the computer light could slip under their eyelids and rouse them from sleep.

The older boy, Steven, had graduated from Castle High School the year before. Ted had wanted to send him to college, but the family's financial problems had thwarted that plan. Shy and chubby the way Ted had been in his teens, Steven stayed at home, playing computer games. His younger brother, Eric, was a junior at Castle. Lean, outspoken, and rebellious, Eric argued frequently with his mother. With Ted, though, he tried to be compliant, and he often wished aloud that his father could spend more time at home.

Ted logged in to his favorite site, Sexyfriends.com. A few years before, he'd discovered it while visiting another sex site. Above the link had been these words: "Tired of trying so hard to make a dollar? Get some relief—and an eyeful—at Sexy Friends!" It cost him $35 a month, but for little more than a dollar a day, he could watch videos, chat with women, email as many of them as he wanted, and create a personal gallery of images and video clips.

He went to his mailbox to see if anyone had left a message. Two women had written to say they weren't interested in corresponding with a married man. The third one said she didn't care about his marital status and was happy to meet him. How about a fast-food place at a shopping mall in 'Aiea? This Saturday at 10:30 would be good for her. Ted stared at the message, surprised. Women had suggested before that they meet, but this was the first time the invitation had appeared so soon. All he'd sent her was his standard message: "I'm a married man that likes to email. I want to make friends. What would you like to talk about?"

He decided he wouldn't respond. *It's like accepting a cannibal's invitation to dinner,* he thought. *Who knows what'll be on the menu?* He opened a new tab and checked his Gmail account. There were two messages from his girlfriend, Claudia. After reading the first one, he wrote back, "I miss you too, hon. I wake up without you next to me, and my arms ache for you. I'll try to come over tomorrow night." Claudia's second message reminded him that she'd be going to a concert on Sunday afternoon. He read it without replying, then went back to Sexy Friends.

He started looking at the new pictures. A young woman—around eighteen, he guessed—was lying on a bed, propping herself up so that he could get a good look at her breasts. She lay at an angle to the camera so that he could see her lower body as well. He wrote a comment: "What a nice ass. Better than any I've seen—and I've seen plenty." He slowly circled her nipples with his cursor, then followed the outline of her legs and her buttocks. He traced her head and again her whole body, then put the cursor on her lips. He looked at a couple dozen more women, then came back to her. With long, straight hair, young brown eyes, and a full, dark-red mouth, she was by far the best. He put her picture in his personal gallery.

He opened another tab and checked the joint bank account he had with his wife, Ellie. Scanning the list of payments and withdrawals, he again remarked how quickly a $2,000 paycheck could disappear every two weeks. He paid a few bills, noting the balance: $137. His individual checking account wasn't doing any better. Hot dogs, peanut-butter sandwiches, and boiled eggs for another two weeks. He turned the laptop off, rose from the small secondhand desk, and walked to his room.

Originally a large storage closet on the second floor of the home, it had been converted into a bedroom. Plastic bags were piled in one corner, and a cabinet sat in another. He opened two small windows near the ceiling, letting in the night air, then went through one of the bags. He found a clean T-shirt, but no clean underwear. Steven had taken his underwear again. The kids rarely did the wash, and Ellie never. Ted could get to it only once a week, and by then the hamper was full and dirty laundry lay on the floor.

He went to the bathroom, passing by his daughter's bedroom, dark and empty. He closed the bathroom door, stepping on the clothes that lay on the floor. He pulled off his jeans and his underwear. The underwear had a large wet spot on the crotch. He wadded some toilet tissue and scraped off the sticky fluid. His mechanic's job at the military base made him sweat a lot, so his underwear was damp with perspiration as well. Pulling off his red T-shirt, he glanced down. Though he was smaller than most of the other mechanics and still able to get into tight, cramped spaces to do his work, he was getting thick around the middle. He was five foot nine and edging up toward a hundred and ninety pounds.

That morning, Ellie had hinted that she'd like him to join her in bed, but he'd again ignored her. *What has she given me but shame and heartache?*

They had made love often the first year they met. He thought her the prettiest woman on the campus of the small college they attended, and she thought him sexy, mature, and confident. A Christian, he had been attracted to the mainland college's offerings in theology and liberal arts. After he graduated, he returned home and found a job, living with his parents to save money. When Ellie graduated, he paid for her trip to the islands, and they got married. Soon, however, his confidence turned into arrogance and her warmth and openness into constant need for attention. Then she had a brief affair. He tried to remain loyal despite her betrayal, lies, and reversals of promises, but she continued to flirt with men, saying she was just being friendly. One day the effort backfired, and she was attacked by an elder of their Wahiawā church. Because of the man's high position, she begged Ted not to confront him or retaliate. Hurt and humiliated, Ted concluded she couldn't be reformed, and he began to look for comfort outside the marriage. *She started first*, he reminded himself.

✄

Ted parked his 1978 dark-blue Kawasaki motorcycle, then walked to the large government warehouse where he worked. The second shift started at 2:30, and he was early, as usual. Coming to the locker room, he was surprised to find his supervisor sitting on a chair next to the door.

"Ted, put your stuff away, then come with me. Hurry up." Usually quiet and aloof, Vince Reynaldo seemed irritated, almost hostile. The white-haired Filipino man looked Ted directly in the eye, as if he were a stranger who'd trespassed on government property.

Ted went to his locker and quickly slipped off his backpack, setting it on the floor. Then he removed his helmet, gloves, and jacket, pulling the ID out of the breast pocket and clipping it to his T-shirt. He put his things away, closed the locker, and joined his supervisor at the door.

Vince walked ahead to the unit's office, a large trailer parked in a corner of the building. He climbed up the three steps to the front door, then led

Ted to the far room. Holding the door open, he let Ted enter first. Ted was surprised to see two men in aloha shirts and pressed trousers sitting at the conference table. The younger man stood up and showed Ted a large, shiny badge: around the top of the crest were the words DEPARTMENT OF JUSTICE, and around the bottom, FEDERAL BUREAU OF INVESTIGATION. The older man remained seated, pulled out a leather holder, and showed his badge to Ted as if it were nothing important.

"Ted," the supervisor said, "these two men would like to talk to you." Ted hesitated, unsure if Vince would stay.

After a few seconds of silence, the older man motioned to Ted to sit at the table. Vince pulled out a chair and sat across from them.

"Mr. Koga, my name is Wynn Johnson," he said, his voice accented by a Southern drawl. "This is my partner, Stanford Park. We would like to ask you a few questions."

Ted nodded.

"Agent Park and I are investigating the assault and attempted murder of a woman who lived in downtown Honolulu. She was a member of an online group called *Sexy Friends*. Have you heard of it, Mr. Koga?"

Ted stared at the agent. His heart started pounding. He felt he couldn't hear anything, and yet he knew what the agent had said.

"Have you ever visited Sexyfriends.com, Mr. Koga?"

Senior to most of his co-workers, Ted was in his late fifties and tried to keep to himself, hoping to avoid personal conflicts. He worked hard to be a model employee, deciding it was the best path to job security. Now he wondered if he should answer the agent's question honestly. He looked across at Vince. Anyone watching the supervisor would think that he was indifferent to what was going on, but Ted knew the opposite was true: Vince was hearing every word, pause, and breath.

Ted looked down, unable to answer.

Park opened a manila folder lying on the table and pulled out a document. It appeared to be a copy of a credit-card statement. "Mr. Koga, do you recognize this document?"

Ted felt like jumping up and running away as fast as he could, but he could not move. His eyes scanned the document, going down the lines. He felt as if he were descending a ladder.

"Is this statement yours, Mr. Koga?"

Ted nodded numbly. The investigators had gotten access to one of his accounts and printed out the statement for the previous month. Amid the payments for food, tools, motorcycle parts, gas, and household items were purchases his family knew nothing about.

Park pointed to a line with his pen. "On May 10, you paid $35 to Eros Unlimited, the parent company of Sexy Friends. This is for a monthly membership fee, is it not?"

Ted looked at the agent. "Sorry...you mean...?"

"Let me rephrase the question. Sexy Friends has a monthly membership fee of $35 for people who wish to access its site. Did you pay Eros Unlimited $35 on May 10 for a basic monthly membership?"

Ted nodded. Vince had heard some of this already, he guessed.

"Mr. Reynaldo provided us with a copy of your work schedule for the period covered by this statement. We see that even though you live in Kāneʻohe and work in Pearl City, you had several charges at establishments downtown. Do you frequent the businesses in that area, Mr. Koga?"

"Can you tell me why I should answer that?" Ted's face turned dark red.

Johnson repeated Park's question. "Do you frequent the businesses in that area?"

Ted scoffed. "These are diners, supermarkets, hardware stores, gas stations. Not a crime to go there, is it?"

"Not a crime, Mr. Koga, but withholding information could be. Please answer the question," Johnson said evenly.

Ted never swore, but he felt like cursing the man. "Yes," he said with great effort, "I go to those places."

"On May 3," Park continued, "the victim corresponded with another site member. She suggested they meet at a fast-food place in 'Aiea. We believe that you were the person she wrote to. Is that right, Mr. Koga?"

The investigator flipped over the statement to another document. It was a printout of a page at Sexyfriends.com. At the top was a banner: a wide, narrow picture of a nude woman lying on her side. Below it was a silhouette enclosed in a frame, and beneath the frame some letters in bold: GREYWOLF. Next to the image was a sentence: "I would like to make friends with women."

"Is this your profile page, Mr. Koga?"

At Sexy Friends, Ted enjoyed encounters with women who were intense and eager for sexual contact, yet noncommittal. He liked the excitement of trolling, of writing to dozens of women a week, but he never exchanged messages with a woman for long.

Johnson again repeated Park's question: "Is this your profile page, Mr. Koga?"

Ted nodded again. The hands on the wall clock seemed to have stopped.

"On May 3, the victim wrote to you. She suggested the two of you meet. She named a place, a day, and a time. Did you two meet, Mr. Koga?"

"No, no, that wasn't me. We didn't meet."

"You did write to her, though. Didn't you, Mr. Koga?"

"I...yes...I wrote first. I didn't write back."

"What did you write, Mr. Koga?...Mr. Koga?" Ted didn't answer, so Park pulled out another sheet. "You wrote, 'I'm a married man that likes to email. I want to make friends. What would you like to talk about?' What did these conversations usually consist of, Mr. Koga?"

"Uh...oh, just the kinds of conversations you might have at a bus stop, waiting for a bus."

Vince snorted.

"Did you talk about your work here at the military base?"

"No."

"Never?"

"No, never."

Park stared at Ted. Vince looked away.

The questioning ended abruptly. "Thank you for meeting with us, Mr. Koga. Depending on how our investigation goes, we may contact you again."

"Thousands of guys belong to that site. Why do you have to question *me*?" Ted demanded.

Johnson looked at him and answered as if he were instructing a junior employee. His heavy-lidded eyes were impassive, as if to counter the effect of his words. "Mr. Koga, you work at a military installation. In order to do so, you need security clearance—and in order to work on defense systems, you need to qualify at a high level and maintain that qualification. When you became a federal employee, you were investigated, as you know. Among other things, the federal government had to determine if you were subject to bribery or blackmail. You eventually received clearance."

"What in the world does visiting a website have to do with security clearance?"

"In our investigation of this case, we looked at the records of many men, yes. Yours got our attention because of your work. Suppose you and the victim met, she found out what you did—she already knew you were married, right?—and decided to blackmail you. We need to be sure that there was no danger of the security of this base being compromised by you."

In response to Ted's silence, the agents stood up, ending the meeting. They shook hands with Vince and left.

Ted looked down at the table, unable to move. Who was he thirty minutes ago? Had he been Ted Koga, member of unit 38, next in line to be a work leader and then, some of his co-workers said, foreman? He tried to remember where he lived, how he'd gotten to work. He couldn't summon a single image. He thought of two boys somewhere and had the odd feeling they were watching him.

Finally he stood up and smacked the table with the flat of his hand, making the clock on the wall jump.

✗

Claudia was confused by the bookmark in her computer's browser. She had met Ted three years before at the dating site and couldn't understand why a bookmark for it was appearing now. She opened the browsing history, reading dozens of URLs to see if msmatch.com was listed. She saw it had been visited several times, the last at 4:10 on Sunday, when she'd been at the concert. She looked at the surrounding entries and saw the addresses for sites she knew Ted frequented: his bank, Amazon.com, One Main Financial. So, she realized, in between checking his accounts, he'd gone to the dating site.

When she first met Ted, he told her he was estranged from his wife and would leave her from time to time and live somewhere else. Only in the last six months had he confessed it was a lie: he'd never been separated from his wife. Claudia had forgiven him, believing he'd eventually divorce Ellie. Now it was obvious that if he were going to do that, it would not be soon—and not after he'd considered other women. *What a fool I've been!* She grabbed her keys and walked to the front door, avoiding the hallway mirror lest she see the self-reproach and contempt that had her on fire. She went to the basement of her building and found a large cardboard box. In half an hour she had everything of his—as well as his gifts to her— packed and loaded in her car.

✗

Ted thought about the events of the past month. He was reading the paper, hoping to find something about the investigation.

Nothing had been disclosed to his family, and he had said nothing. His wife and sons questioned him several times about his sudden moodiness. He said his getting older and being prone to injury were responsible: too many bruises, lacerations, pulled muscles, chronic aches. He was also at home more. The defense department was cutting back to save money, he explained, so there would be no overtime or emergency work for several months. In actuality, Vince had removed him from the list of people eligible for extra work.

Claudia had also written him. He hadn't been attracted to her when they'd first met, but he discovered that he craved the excitement the affair brought his dull life. She was five feet tall and had shoulder-length hair, which she dyed black, and liked to wear nice clothes and high heels. Holding her and smelling her perfume made him feel that he wasn't the loser he often thought he was. Her message said she was donating his things to the Salvation Army: clothes, shoes, gadgets, computer software, books, and personal items she'd bought for him or he'd bought for her. He replied that he would never go back to the dating site—that bookmarking it had been an accident—but she ignored his promise. "Send me my keys through the mail, you asshole!" she wrote back. Then she blocked him on her email and her phone.

Vince no longer spoke to him unless he had to, and his co-workers seemed to know something. One of them, he heard, had seen the agents coming out of the trailer—then Ted and, a few minutes later, Vince. The co-worker must have spoken to the supervisor. Ted was sure Vince hadn't given him any details, but maybe the little he had said had tipped things in a certain direction.

Ted lay down, but couldn't sleep.

He got up and went to his sons' bedroom. The room was brightly lit and warm. Eric had taped one of his pencil drawings to the wall by his bed: a Terminator figure, battle scarred and missing an eye. Steven had a *Star Trek* poster by his bed. The boys were listening to music and talking. Ted sat down at the computer and went to a science site they all liked. He had done well in math and science when he was in high school. Hearing the site's theme music, his sons got up and stood by him. As he gazed into their faces, he thought, *They are wonderful kids. I was just like them at one time. Just like them!* he wanted to shout to the world.

✄

"Ted," his supervisor said to his back as he opened his locker. "Those guys want to talk to you again."

Ted followed the Filipino man to the trailer, passing some of his co-workers. *Questions. More. From everybody,* he thought.

"Ted is here."

Both men stayed seated. Agent Park hailed him and motioned him to sit down.

"Mr. Koga, we want to ask you more questions."

"OK."

Park handed him a color printout of a snapshot. In the foreground were four people.

"This is a picture of the woman who went by the name Ginger Wong. Do you recognize her?"

Ted looked at the printout carefully, trying to remember if he'd seen her at Sexyfriends.com.

"No, never saw her before."

"Are you sure, Mr. Koga?"

"Yes...I'm sure."

"Do you recognize the men in the picture?"

Three men were at the table with Wong, one sitting next to her and the other two across.

"No, never saw them before either."

"What about this man?" The agent pointed to a fourth man sitting in a corner, next to the men's room.

Ted saw the profile of an Asian man with graying hair. He was laughing, and Ted could see that he didn't have a small, flat nose as most Asians did, but a wide, fleshy nose. Ted stared at the picture, unable to accept what he saw.

"That is you, Mr. Koga, is it not?"

Ted moved his chair sharply, attempting to rise.

"Mr. Koga, please don't get up. Our questioning is not done."

"But *I'm* done, and I need to get to work."

"Ted, *sit there!*" Vince said.

Looking at the three men, Ted exhaled deeply, but the worry was still lodged in his chest.

"Can you explain how you happen to be in this picture, Mr. Koga?... Mr. Koga?"

Ted had lost the power of speech—or the need for it. He felt everything he wanted to communicate was being said by his eyes. Couldn't the men read what was in his eyes?

He shook his head. "N-n-no," he stuttered. "I...I can't...Where did this picture come from?"

"Wong had a Facebook page with many friends, most of them guys. One of them had this photograph on his page, in an album labeled 'Bars.'"

"I don't go to bars." No one responded, so Ted repeated himself. "I don't go to bars. My Christian values—"

"Your *what?!*" Vince said.

Ted looked down. "Our teachings don't allow drinking. It's prohibited."

"But going to sex sites is OK?" Vince asked, his eyes wide.

"No, it's not," Ted said, still looking down.

"Yeah, right. You don't drink, but you go to sex sites and cheat on your wife. *Christian values*—what a joke."

"Mr. Reynaldo, *please*," Johnson said, "let us do the questioning."

Vince sat back in his chair and folded his arms. Ted could read everything in his look.

Park spoke. "The caption for the photograph says it was taken in the Pink & Drink Bar near the airport. We examined your account statements but could find no purchases at this bar—"

"*Of course not!*" Ted exploded. "That's because I never went there!"

"Mr. Koga," Johnson said, "you could have paid with cash, correct? Sir, let me remind you that if you perjure yourself, this serious situation will get much worse. It's crucial that you be completely honest with us. Is that clear, Mr. Koga?"

Ted tried to swallow, but his throat had closed up and he felt like he was choking. Unable to speak, he looked at Johnson and simply nodded.

"Mr. Koga," Johnson said firmly, "did you go to the Pink & Drink Bar?"

"No."

"Did you ever meet Ginger Wong face-to-face?"

"No."

"Did you ever attempt to contact her, other than sending your initial message?"

"No."

"Thank you, Mr. Koga. There are no more questions today. We will be in touch. Good day, Mr. Koga…Mr. Reynaldo."

The two men left, Johnson leading. Ted sat at the table with his supervisor.

Standing up, Vince said, "The base commander has been getting reports on the investigation. Just letting you know—in case you were wondering."

✄

Vince handed Ted an envelope as he sat in front of his locker, lacing up his steel-toed work boots. Opening it, Ted found a letter from the commander.

Dear Mr. Koga:

For the last eight years, you have been an exemplary member of the civilian workforce. However, your involvement in the continuing investigation is a matter of concern. I have met with the investigators, reviewed their reports, and discussed the situation with Human Resources. Our decision follows.

You are hereby put on paid leave beginning Monday and continuing for the next four weeks. During this time, you will meet with Charlene Ho'okano, PhD, of the Civilian Employee Assistance Program. Her schedule has been cleared to accommodate fifty-minute sessions with you at 0900 on Monday, Wednesday, and Friday.

Please do not fail to attend these sessions; if emergencies arise, contact Dr. Ho'okano or your supervisor, Vince Reynaldo, immediately. Failure to do so will result in suspension. At the end of the four-week period, Dr. Ho'okano will submit a report and we will take appropriate action.

Please also be reminded that because this is an official matter, all details are to remain confidential.

Ted reread the letter. He understood that his security clearance was at risk of being revoked and if that happened, he would lose his job. The sessions with the counselor were no doubt meant to determine if he were fit to continue working.

Every day, he had reined in his frustration with his bosses and co-workers, said nothing about the instances of favoritism he suspected, tried to work alongside the testy, competitive men who were younger by decades, to shrug off the disappointments of not being selected for promotions or better-paying jobs. Even though he'd gone to college, the school was unaccredited, so his four years couldn't be applied to any position requiring a higher-education degree. When his co-workers had tried to get him to join them on trips to bars or strip clubs, he'd always said no. They could count on his saying no to their excursions. They could count on his choosing to be different—to be, they thought, a good man. He never wavered.

What would he tell his family this time? *Our unit is being investigated for employee theft. Each person has to take a month off while he is investigated thoroughly.* Would Ellie and the boys believe the new lie?

⚡

Charlene Hoʻokano's office was on the third floor of the Human Resources building. One of the older buildings on the base, it was built of wood, was painted a light brown, and had high ceilings, wide stairways, and linoleum-tile floors. Rather than take the old elevator, Ted climbed the stairs to the third floor. A row of windows on his left filled the corridor with morning light. Coming to her office, he knocked softly on the door.

"E komo mai. Please come in," a low female voice responded.

Ted entered the plain room. The desk was parallel to the back wall, and on it was a vase with a cutting of pink plumeria. A slender woman sat behind the desk, and as Ted approached her, she rose, extending her hand. "Charlene Hoʻokano," she said.

"Ted Koga," he said awkwardly. Her hand was soft and warm.

She was tall, at least a couple inches taller than he was. Her short hair was graying, and she wore a Hawaiian bracelet on her left wrist and a jade one on her right. He guessed she was in her late forties, but she could have been older. Though he felt self-conscious, he couldn't help staring at her face. Her eyes were a deep green.

Masking his awkwardness, he said, "You always work with the lights off?"

"I can see people just as well in natural light—most of the time any-way—and I find they tend to be more relaxed if the room doesn't feel so much like an office."

"Makes sense," he responded.

The doctor had a manila folder open on her desk, and Ted guessed that the label on the tab had his name. He had expected that she would review records of the investigation, but he felt ashamed nonetheless. He wondered when the circle of review would stop growing.

"Mr. Koga, before we begin our session, I'd like you to fill out these forms."

"What forms?"

"There are three questionnaires here. Standard forms used by therapists in their analysis. Each is only two or three pages long and should take you just a few minutes to complete. Please do not dwell on the questions; just respond naturally, selecting the answer that seems best to you."

"Will these go in that folder?"

"Yes."

"Then everyone will see them?"

"They are only for use in our sessions. They will be kept confidential unless there is something in them that I feel should be shared."

"Not much incentive to be honest then, is there?"

"Mr. Koga, we can't know the answers before we ask the questions. I will use the information to help you. My intention—and the reason these sessions were arranged—is to help you."

"Unless I'm a criminal." The doctor returned his gaze without changing her expression. "Can I make a request too? Stop calling me Mr. Koga. I don't deserve it. For the kind of man I am, Ted will do fine."

"As you wish," she replied. "And please call me Charlene."

Filling out the forms with a pencil, he could see they were variations on a theme: sex addiction. The first asked about sexual practices, the second about fantasies and desires, and the third about use of printed materials, videotapes, and Internet sites. Clutching the pencil, he tried to fill out the forms quickly, but several questions stumped him and he had to stop to consider the answers.

He pushed the forms across the desk and slammed down the pencil.

Charlene put the sheets in the folder and closed it.

"Aren't you going to look at them?"

"I will; when I see you again, we will talk about the forms. For now, I'd like to ask you some questions."

Ted waited.

Charlene picked up a sheet sitting on her desk. "Please tell me about your wife, Eileen Koga née Bergen. Your personnel record says she was born in 1962 and that she's a secretary."

"My wife is a secretary to the pastor of a church in Kāne'ohe. We've been married for thirty years."

"And you have two teenaged sons, Steven and Eric, and a daughter, Gwen?"

"Yeah, the boys live at home. Gwen is twenty-three. She lives on her own."

"Gwen's occupation is not listed here. How does Gwen support herself?"

"I don't know."

"You don't know?"

"No." Ted shifted in his chair.

"Because…"

"I have no idea where she is or what she's doing. Ellie and I lost touch with her. Actually…we believe she's on drugs."

"Tell me about Gwen, please." Charlene started taking notes, and Ted noticed that she wrote with her left hand.

"She and Ellie had a close relationship. I don't think it was healthy. They were always doing things together—like friends or sisters instead of mother and daughter. Gwen was a smart girl, got As in elementary school. When she got to intermediate school, her mom started to teach her how to manipulate guys.

"In high school, she stayed out late, got into trouble, fought with us about her clothes, her grades. After she graduated, she got involved with a guy who drank a lot and got violent when he was drunk. She flirted with other guys, making him jealous, and he slapped her around. She eventually started to hit back, but they stayed together for a while, maybe six months. Then she moved out of their place and started seeing other people. But he was always in the background, calling her, trying to reconnect. Two years ago, he followed her in his car as she was leaving her job. She was a restaurant hostess. He tried to drive her off the road. She lost control of her car and hit an elderly couple. The man moved in front of his wife to protect her. They ended up in the hospital, in critical condition. We tried to get Gwen to file charges against her ex, but she was afraid. She told the police some nut tried to force her off the road."

"What happened to the couple?"

"They eventually recovered, but it was very tough for Gwen. The man almost died. Both of them were permanently disabled. We brought Gwen home, but there wasn't much we could do for her. She hardly ate, cried a lot. One day I came home and found my wife hysterical. Gwen had cut her wrists several times with a razor blade—not deep enough to really hurt herself, but there was blood on her arms and clothes. We took her to the emergency room, and they put her in the psychiatric ward. She stayed there four days, then came home. The next day, she swallowed half a bottle of pills the doctor prescribed, and we had to take her back to the hospital to get her stomach pumped. The morning after that, she took off."

"I see...Have you seen her since then?"

"My wife thinks she's seen Gwen standing outside the house—actually, just her shadow on the living-room curtains. Maybe she was peeking in. Who knows. I haven't seen her myself. She used to call once in a while, asking for money, but we stopped giving it to her. She was smart, coming up with all kinds of reasons why she needed the money. We eventually figured out she was using it to buy drugs. Sometimes when she called, she sounded high and didn't make sense. She'd repeat herself or ask some weird question...You understand why I didn't want to bring that up, right?"

"Yes, of course. As a federal worker, you'd be subject to an investigation if it came out."

"Charlene—"

"I will not add that to my session notes," she said, giving him a look. "It's mere speculation—isn't it, Ted?"

"Yeah, right," he said, his voice fading, "just speculation."

Charlene sat in silence for a minute, then asked, "What was the effect of this situation on your marriage?"

"My wife blamed me, of course. Everything was all my fault. If I hadn't been so angry, rigid, strict, Gwen wouldn't have turned out the way she did."

"And how did you see things?"

"Gwen was almost a carbon copy of her mom: pretty, a flirt; manipulative, greedy, insecure. Her mother had groomed her to use men the same way she uses them."

"Uses them? Do you mean uses you—or uses other men?"

"I mean both. Uses me and other guys."

"So your wife—"

"If she likes the guy, she'll hold his hand, kiss him on the lips when she says hello. She'll say how handsome he is…My mother noticed that I would leave family gatherings really mad."

"These gatherings included…?"

"My brothers, their wives and children, sometimes friends."

"And now?"

"Now we no longer go."

"So your mother has witnessed Eileen's behavior too?"

"She and my dad both. My dad was very offended by it. When we'd go visit them, he'd make some excuse to leave so that he didn't have to talk to her."

"And Eileen works for a pastor? That is pretty…atypical behavior for someone working in a church."

"Of course! Ellie doesn't behave that way in front of her boss."

"I see. Well, I'm afraid we have to stop here, Ted. On Wednesday, we'll talk some more about Eileen and Gwen and I'll go over these forms with you."

"OK. Well, I'll see you Wednesday then."

"Goodbye, Ted," she said, rising and extending her hand.

"Goodbye, Charlene." He shook her hand but did not return her smile.

Riding back to Kāne‘ohe on his motorcycle, Ted gripped the handlebars tightly. He thought about his conversation with Charlene and remembered he had indeed seen Gwen. It was at the Pali.

One night, it had been storming, and though the rain had subsided, the Pali Highway was still slick. Like most motorists taking the road over the mountain in the evening, Ted tried to be careful. The Pali was notorious as the site not only of numerous car accidents—including an SUV with wedding guests that crashed into the side of Wilson Tunnel—but also murders, suicides, and a wind so strong it was a local legend. Once Ted got past the residential district of Nuʻuanu, he entered a heavily forested area. Stretching down the middle of the highway was a row of streetlights. The project had been controversial, some people arguing the lights were needed and others saying they undermined the beauty of the Pali. The engineers had compromised by creating a narrow row of lights down the center, just enough to illuminate the road.

Emerging from the tunnel, Ted took a curve too quickly. On the part of the road that snaked down the mountain to the windward side, he felt the rear wheel begin to lose traction and slide over the wet surface. In seconds, the front wheel followed, and the bike darted out from under him. Sparks flew as the left foot peg scraped the asphalt and the bike skidded across the road. It went over the grassy embankment and crashed into the guard rail. Ted tumbled and rolled, landing on the grass.

Seconds later, a car came around the bend, its headlights shining on Ted and the bike. The car pulled over onto the shoulder, and the doors opened. He could hear two people, a man and a woman, trying to talk above the wind. He recognized the woman's voice.

The man helped Ted sit up. "Hey, you OK?"

"I...yeah, I think so."

"Dad...? Is that you?"

"Yes, Gwen." Ted lifted his arm and reached out to her.

She sat back on her haunches, just out of his reach.

"You sure you're OK?" the man repeated, trying to lift off Ted's helmet. "You want us to get help?"

Ted resisted the man's efforts, waving his hands away. "Yeah, I'm fine. I'll be OK, thanks."

The car's headlights shone on the three of them. *Gwen looks so thin*, Ted thought. *Her cheekbones are poking through her face, and her hair is dirty.*

"You need help with your bike?" the man asked.

"No-no, I'm OK. Thanks for stopping. Really appreciate it...Thank you, Gwen."

"OK, Dad," she said. "He's OK," she said to the man.

The two got up and walked back to their car. Ted reached across his chest to see where the fall might have torn his jacket. The elbow of the jacket was ripped open, his skin exposed. When he got home, he would clean the wound and mend the jacket. It had to meet military specs in order for him to ride onto the base, and he couldn't afford $200 for a new jacket.

As the car passed by Ted, Gwen looked at him through the passenger window. She seemed sad or disappointed or unwell. He couldn't tell which.

Slowly, he pushed himself up from the ground. He stood up stiffly, flexing his joints, then walked over to the bike and tried to right it. It was slippery from mud and wet grass, and he wiped off what he could with his gloved hands. He got back on and started the engine, feeling no pain. But he had lain the bike down before and knew that he would soon be hurting from bruised muscles and stiff joints.

Ted wondered if he should mention seeing Gwen to the doctor. He would try to remember to tell her, but maybe it didn't matter. As with the other times he had made an effort to communicate with his daughter, nothing had come of seeing Gwen.

covenants

"Ted," Charlene said when he sat down, "based on the things you told me at our first meeting, I'd like you to fill out one more form."

"What for? Don't you have enough information?"

"Well, I gave you forms that I thought would be relevant to your...situation. But you told me certain things that made me realize there's more to it than I thought. Please, could you fill out this form?" Charlene handed him three sheets and a pencil.

Ted held the form in his hand, scanning the title and first couple of questions. "'Betrayal Bond'?"

"Yes, this is a concept developed by Dr. Patrick Carnes, a pioneer in psychotherapy. Sometimes we develop strong bonds with people who hurt or manipulate us. Such bonds generate other problems, and we often find ourselves trapped, unable to stay in these relationships and unable to leave. Please fill out the form, Ted. I think it will be very helpful."

"OK, you're the boss."

As he read the questions and tried to answer yes or no, memories started to come. Memories swirled around the words, flowed in between the lines, and poured over his hand, making it hard to write...Images of dressing his children and driving them to school...taking second jobs to pay bills...making excuses for his wife...listening to her confession of an affair...people shifting in and out of their lives, attracted at first by her warmth and gregariousness, then repelled by her disclosures...lies, apologies, admissions...listening to the judge who presided over his bankruptcy proceedings...comforting his daughter after she'd been assaulted...slashing a tree with a machete in anger...accusations, threats, counter threats...

Yes or no: it was so easily divided up for these professionals, he thought. They had it all down: case studies, theories, data, experimental models, certificates on the wall that told the world they knew something. But they had learned it all in books and classrooms.

Ted pushed the form across the desk. This time, Charlene picked it up and read it. "Thank you, Ted. This will be very helpful in treating your condition."

"Why don't you call it what it is?"

"Which is?"

"*An addiction!* Are you afraid to use the word or something?"

"There is some debate among people in the medical profession about whether a condition such as yours is an addiction or not. Some therapists feel that it isn't. Others feel that it is and follow the addiction model closely in treating their patients. Since we are at the beginning of our sessions, I want to learn as much as I can before choosing a diagnostic model."

"But you had me fill out these forms."

"Yes, to collect information."

"So you're not biased one way or the other?"

"As I said, the forms provide us with data—data that we can refer to in our sessions. What we do with that information, how we choose to interpret it—that's all part of the effort to help you."

"Or find me guilty."

"Ted, until you make a clear statement of your guilt, that is not our focus here. Now, shall we get to work?" It sounded more like an order than a question.

Ted sat back in his chair and folded his arms.

"I'd like to start with your visits to Sexyfriends.com. These were made daily; is that correct?"

"Most of the time, yes. Every once in a while I couldn't go to the site, but most of the time, yeah. Sometimes a couple times in a day."

"And you spent how many minutes there would you say? Each time you visited, that is."

"Maybe an hour. There was always...a lot to look at."

"And you also wrote to women at the site, saying you were married."

"Yeah."

"Why did you want women to know you were married?"

Ted shifted in his chair and looked away.

"So that they would know you wanted a certain kind of correspondence; is that right?"

"I didn't want them to think I was interested in...in seeing them or anything. Just writing..."

"About sex."

"Yeah, about sex."

"How explicit was this correspondence?"

"What do you mean?"

"Did you talk about dating, relationships? Or did you focus on foreplay, penetration, coitus—intercourse—orgasm?"

"Foreplay and all that."

"And how many women did you write to a week?"

"As many as I could in the time I had."

"So you would write to how many women a week would you say?"

"I don't know. Maybe twenty...I'm not sure."

"And you were a member for how long?"

"Almost three years."

"Are you still a member?"

"Are you kidding? I stopped when I met with the FBI guys."

"Did you ever correspond with women when you were off the site—that is, women you'd met at Sexyfriends?"

"No."

"It was always at the site?"

"Yeah."

"And did you ever pay for additional services?"

"Like?"

"Phone sex, web-cam viewing, that kind of thing."

"I thought about it..."

"But?"

"But I couldn't afford it, to tell you the truth."

"But you would have if you could have afforded it?"

"Well, eventually, yeah...probably."

"And your wife had no inkling of what was going on?"

"She caught me once."

"Visiting the site?"

"I was using the computer and went to a porn site. I didn't know she was nearby. She saw the page when she came to ask me something. We had a big argument about it."

"What did you say?"

"I denied it, of course. I said I accidentally clicked on a link in an email message. I was very embarrassed she caught me, but I wasn't going to admit it. I took the offensive, yelled at her, kicked a chair, knocked it over."

"And how did she react?"

"She cried."

"So you asserted your innocence by going into a rage?"

"Well, yeah, I guess you could put it that way."

"And did that happen often? You two would have an argument, you would become furious, and she would cry?"

"Well, you gotta understand the way we argued, Charlene. Most of the time, she was trying to get her way. I would try to reason with her, but she would interpret that as criticizing her. She'd start to cry, and eventually I would have to back down, say I was sorry."

"But in the case where she caught you, you didn't back down. You said you took the offensive."

"Well, yeah, there wasn't anything else I could do. Otherwise, she would explode."

"So you made her *implode.*"

Ted didn't respond.

"You didn't want to admit the truth."

Ted stayed silent.

"You never would have admitted the truth—"

"I couldn't..."

"Otherwise she would have made you stop—"

"Yeah."

"And you couldn't stop." Charlene looked at him hard.

"No...The truth was...I didn't want to stop."

"Do you have rape fantasies, Ted?"

He didn't reply.

"Do you have fantasies of forcing women to have sex with you against their will?"

Again he said nothing.

Charlene looked up from her note-taking. "Ted, unless you answer no, I may have to interpret your silence as a positive reply."

He sat quietly.

"Do these fantasies involve underaged females?"

"No."

"You have fantasies about forced sex, but they do not involve minors?"

"Yes," he said softly.

"Do you have fantasies about multiple partners?"

Ted looked down. "Yes."

"Anonymous encounters—that is, brief encounters just for sex?"

"Yes."

Charlene made more notes.

"I guess that makes me a pervert, huh?"

"The line between what we recognize as normal and what we deem as perverse is usually drawn outside the imagination."

"Translate into English, please."

"Unless your fantasies interfere with your life—for example, if you have them compulsively to the point where they interfere with work, sleep, and so forth—we don't automatically interpret them as pathological."

"Why are you asking me about them then?"

"I'm trying to complete your psychological profile."

"So I'm not a pervert?"

Charlene ignored the question. "Do you watch videos of women being assaulted, beaten?"

"No."

"In public situations, such as elevator rides with strangers, do you feel tempted to grab, molest, or assault women?"

"No."

"Girls?"

"No."

"Boys?"

Ted shook his head.

"Men?"

"Of course not! I'm not gay," Ted said with disgust.

"Homosexual behavior falls within the normal range, Ted. It is not in itself a pathology."

"My religious teachings say differently."

"What do they say about sex sites and trolling for anonymous sex partners?"

Ted started to reply, then stopped and looked down at his hands. "I thought God would forgive me."

"As he watched you visit these sex sites, you thought he was forgiving you?"

"I thought he would...look away."

"You—of all the people in the world—he would pardon from his gaze?"

"There are lots of guys like me, you know. Other Christians, I mean."

"Religion often figures in the personal history of sex offenders."

"I'm not a sex offender! I'm not a criminal! I didn't do anything that millions of guys all over the U.S. don't do every day."

"The U.S. has the highest rate of sex-related crimes in the world. Some social scientists believe that it's no coincidence we are also the world's leading consumer society. Sex as a commodity for recreation and entertainment is traded thousands of times an hour."

"I wasn't trading it—I mean, I wasn't buying it for...for entertainment only. I was very lonely and angry. Ellie had an affair soon after we married, and she was always friendly with other men, touching them, comparing them to me. When Gwen was fifteen, she was attacked by a classmate. Attempted rape. We saw a family therapist, but it was a terrible time. Ellie and I stopped having sex. Gwen slept with her because she was afraid."

"Your daughter slept with your wife?"

"Yes."

"How long did that go on?"

"Till Gwen was eighteen. She met a guy soon after she graduated from high school, and she moved in with him."

Charlene shook her head, making notes. "And where did you sleep, Ted?"

"When we moved to the Kāneʻohe house, I converted a walk-in storage closet into a small bedroom. I had my things in there, mostly in plastic bags, and slept on a folding mattress."

"So Gwen slept with your wife till she graduated from high school?"

"Yes."

"What was their relationship like?"

"As I said, they were friends, buddies."

"Where did Gwen keep her clothes? Did she move them into the master bedroom?"

"No, she had her own room. The two girls—Ellie and Gwen—would spend a lot of time in each other's rooms, though."

"I notice you call them girls. Why?"

"They were like sisters. Sometimes they worked together to deceive me, keep secrets. I felt like their dad instead of Ellie's husband."

"I see. You mentioned seeing a therapist when Gwen was attacked. Did you file charges against the boy?"

"No, we didn't. We figured it would traumatize Gwen even more."

"Can you tell me what happened with the therapist? What did he or she say?"

"It was a Christian therapist. Ellie found him through the church. At first, they were friendly, and I felt...left out. But as time went on, he began to understand my side of things and we ended up becoming friends. Then Ellie had a falling out with him and stopped the counseling."

"Tell me about that, please."

"He told her that her relationship with Gwen was not healthy. They were too much like peers, he said, and Ellie needed to be a parent. She got really emotional in one session and told me she was not going back."

"What about you? Did you continue seeing the therapist?"

"No, I couldn't."

"Why not?"

"Because Ellie would feel I was betraying her. I always had to take her side against other people."

Charlene nodded. "Otherwise you'd have another argument?"

"Yeah. It would go on and on until I finally agreed with her."

"Were you regularly going to porn sites by then?"

"Yes."

"So did you share that with the therapist?"

"No. The focus was on Gwen and how to help her—and the family dynamics. The doctor did counsel me about my anger problem—"

"You had a problem with anger?"

"Yeah. I would get really mad: break things, punch things, kick them. I never hurt anybody, except when I spanked the kids, and that was just once in a while."

"So the therapist counseled you on anger management?"

"Yeah, he had me take a course too."

"And did that help?"

"Yeah, but not in the long run. We had so many problems that I couldn't help it. When I was working part-time for the church, one of the elders attacked Ellie. She was very friendly with him for a while—giving him hugs, compliments, little gifts, like things she'd baked. Then one day when I wasn't home, she asked him to come over to fix something in the house. When I got home, she was very upset and told me he grabbed her and tried to put his hand in her clothes. She pushed him away and yelled at him to leave. I wanted to beat him up, but she begged me not to do anything. We never confronted him, but he could tell from my behavior that I knew. He set me up to get fired, bad-mouthing me and accusing me of things I didn't do. I really needed the job. My income from the hardware store was not enough.

"It was too much: the attack on Ellie after I warned her not to flirt with guys; being framed by someone in a high position at the church; getting fired; losing income we needed. And no one at the church stood by me; not a single friend even talked to me after that. I felt like I had a big hole in my chest where my heart used to be.

"I turned to porn to keep me going. It was the only thing that could take my mind off what I was going through. Soon it was the only thing that made me happy—that I wanted. Work two jobs, work around the clock—I'd do anything to get it."

"So there was no one for you to reach out to?"

"No."

"What about your parents?"

"One night, my dad called and asked me to stop sharing my problems with them. He said it was making my mother upset. She wasn't in good health—she just had a mastectomy and was very depressed."

"So you kept it all inside?"

"Yes."

"I see..." Charlene sighed deeply, then made more notes. "Well, I'm afraid we have to stop for today...Ted, you may not feel that anyone cares, but I do. I care. I care about what happened."

Unable to respond, Ted sat in silence. "Thank you," he finally said, avoiding her gaze as he stood up. "See you next week."

As Ted walked down the stairway, Charlene's words came back to him. *Viewing pornography is a complex form of masturbation...The U.S. has the highest number of sex crimes in the world...Many sex offenders have religion in their background...The reason you continued to view pornography is different from the reason you started...*Ted wanted to get on his motorcycle and race down the freeway. How often he had done that to burn off feelings of frustration, helplessness, and shame. Charlene wouldn't know what that felt like. How could she know? A comfortable middle-class woman with a white-collar job. She'd never felt the kind of self-pity that kills.

He stopped on the landing, rested his hand on the rail. Once he had two little boys and a girl. He was everything to them, and they were everything to him. He wanted to teach them about the world and the ways that children grow straight, tall, and good in the eyes of the Lord. But he himself had failed. He had been the one to lie down with temptation. And he had stayed there.

games of power

Soon after she finished breakfast with Steven and Eric, Ellie went back upstairs to the master bedroom. Ted sat in the living room, watching the TV.

The old gray tabby lay sleeping in the bedroom doorway. Stepping over him, Ellie walked to the executive desk a friend had given her the year before. Lillian was buying a new one for her real estate office, and Ellie had said she could use a good desk. When she had told Ted about it, he pointed out that the desk would take up a third of the room, forcing everything but the bed into narrow spaces along the wall. Ellie asked Lillian to have the desk delivered anyway, insisting to Ted that it would make her more productive. Made of hardwood and varnished, the desk was where she opened mail, wrote checks, made to-do lists for her sons and husband, browsed magazines and catalogues, wrote to friends, and studied her Bible.

A stack of folded laundry sat on the desk, and she moved it onto a box on the floor. She turned on the computer, went to her Facebook page, and read a message from Pastor Edward. He reminded her to strengthen her faith by renewing her trust in God: "When Ted is ready to be by your side again, the good Lord will return him to you." The same advice as before: Ellie could always depend on Pastor Edward to repeat himself.

She logged in to her email account, wondering if there would be a message from Joseph, a man she'd met at the church social the Friday before. She had offered to show him around, saying she remembered how it felt to be newly arrived in Hawai'i and so far from the mainland.

Her co-worker Lina had written her instead. A file was attached to the message: an invitation to a birthday party for her son, Francis, a sophomore at Windward Community College. Lina was very proud of Francis, the first in her family to attend college. She'd raised him and his younger sister, Renee, by herself. Overprotective and doting, Lina annoyed Ellie by talking about her children constantly. Ellie's face hardened. *None of my children will ever go to college, and they're much smarter! If only Ted was a better husband...*Ellie thought again of calling his parents, but Ted had told her not to call.

Don't phone my parents; they don't want to be involved...Don't phone me when I'm at work; you can't reach me anyway...Don't send me long email messages...Don't argue with me in front of the kids...Don't take my things without asking me first...Don't talk to me about your job; you never listen to my advice anyway...Don't spend money on things we don't need...Don't ask people for favors; ask me first...Don't talk to anybody about our problems...Don't make a major decision without consulting me..."He has so many rules," she complained to her friends, "I feel like I'm still living with my parents!"

The next message was from her dentist's office, giving her alternative dates and times for her appointment. Could she please select the most convenient one and get back to them? Ellie searched for a pen on the desk, then in the drawers. Finding none, she looked around and spied one beneath the desk. She picked it up and wrote the dates and times on the back of an envelope, adding a note to get back to the dentist's office. Heavy footsteps sounded on the stairs. "Steven, is that you?"

"Yeah, Mom."

"Steven, the carpet in here is very dirty. Can you vacuum it like I asked you to?"

"Yeah, Mom."

"And don't forget your room."

"Yeah, Mom."

A few minutes later, Ellie could hear the computer blasting from the boys' room: low-pitched sounds of bombs and high-pitched sounds of laser guns. After browsing her friends' Facebook pages and seeing if she could find any news of Gwen, she decided to remind Steven about the cleaning. Stumbling over the cat as it moved toward her, she knocked over the wastebasket. The contents spilled onto the floor, adding wadded tissue, torn envelopes, store receipts, and strands of light-brown hair to the dirty carpet. "Good lord," she muttered.

Walking into the boys' room, she saw that Steven was hunched over his computer, wearing his headphones and vigorously moving the controls of a game box. He was completely absorbed and didn't notice her. She walked closer and looked at the screen. A female figure in a white jumpsuit was fighting a male opponent dressed in black. The male was firing a laser gun, and every time a shot made contact with the female, it blew off some part of her clothing. When she was nearly nude, the attacker jumped down and, wielding a sword, cut off her head. Blood gushed onto the ground, and the man kicked her body into a trough full of other headless females. Sensing someone behind him, Steven said, "Eric, come look. I beat your score!" He turned around with a look of triumph and glee.

Seeing the look, Ellie raised her hand and slapped him across the face. He jumped to his feet and raised his arm to strike back.

"*Steven!*" Ted yelled.

The boy dropped his arm and staggered backward, bumping against the computer table.

"What's going on here?!"

"Your son is watching violent porn!" Ellie said, trembling with rage.

"It's just a stupid *game*, Mom!"

"No, it's not! You call shooting off a girl's clothes until she's naked and then chopping off her head a *game*?!"

"It's just for fun!"

"*Fun*?! That's what you call *fun*?!"

"Steven, move away from the computer."

"Why?"

"Because I asked you to." Ted spoke in a monotone. "*Right now*, Steven."

The boy moved aside, and Ted walked up to the computer, glanced at the screen, and turned the machine off. He started disassembling the game equipment.

"Dad, what are you doing?"

"Removing the game box, Steven. You and Eric are grounded for a month. No games except the ones approved by your mom and me. That clear, Steven?"

The boy looked down, mumbling to himself.

"What are you doing, Dad?" Everyone turned to see Eric standing in the doorway.

Ted faced the boy. "Eric, you and Steven are grounded. No violent games. No games at all except ones approved by your mom and me."

"But why do you have to take the game box?"

"For your own good, Eric. When your mom and I are convinced you boys can control yourselves, I'll put it back."

Eric clenched his fists. "And how will you know that, Dad?"

"We'll know, Eric. Somehow."

Eric walked to the closet and slammed his fist into the door, breaking the wood.

"*Eric!*"

The boy turned to face his father, then pivoted on his foot and punched the door again, making a hole in it.

"*Eric!*" Ellie yelled, crying. "Please don't...*don't.*" Ellie fell to her knees.

"Steven, take your mom to her room and close the door."

The older boy didn't move.

"*Now, Steven!*"

Steven walked awkwardly to his mother, bent down, and touched her on the shoulder. "Mom, come. Let's go to your room, OK?...Mom, please?"

Ellie didn't respond. Then tentatively she raised her hand, and Steven clutched it, slipped his other hand under her elbow, and slowly rose, bringing her with him. When she was standing, he put his arm around her waist and walked her to the master bedroom. She moved toward the bed and lay down, lifting her knees and wrapping her arms around her legs. She started sobbing.

"Don't cry, Mom. Dad will take care of everything." Steven put a box of tissue on the night table and pulled the blanket over her. He walked to the door, softly closed it, and returned to his room.

"Steven, stay with your mom."

"Dad, she's—"

"Steven, do as I say, son."

The boy returned to the master bedroom and closed the door behind him.

Ted turned toward the lean figure of Eric. He sensed the anger pulsing through the boy from head to foot. Eric lunged at his father, and Ted grabbed his arm and twisted it behind his back. Then he wrapped his left arm around the boy's neck and put him in a chokehold. Eric struggled helplessly.

"OK, Eric, are we going to talk this way?! Or man-to-man?"

With all his strength, the boy screamed and tried to break free.

"OK, we'll do it your way! We'll fight! Is that what you want? Huh, son?"

Eric finally relented. Ted relaxed his hold, ready to grab him again. The boy brought his hand to his eyes, wiping away tears. His body was limp.

"Sorry...sorry, Dad," he said, speaking barely above a whisper.

"It's OK, son. I forgive you...Sit down. Let's talk..."

The boy collapsed on his bed.

"Eric, your mom and I can't let you and Steven play those violent games."

"They aren't violent, Dad. They're fun."

"Your reaction tells me they're more than fun. Isn't that right, son?"

The boy didn't respond.

"I'm going to remove the game stuff and lock it up, OK? Later today we'll have a family meeting and set down some rules."

"Dad, this isn't necessary. It's a whole lot of trouble—"

"Eric, your mom and I will decide what's necessary. When you're standing in my shoes, you can make the rules, OK?"

The boy turned away and pummeled his pillow. Ted walked back to the computer, gathered up the equipment, and walked out of the room.

⚄

That Sunday, Ellie went to church. After the service, she saw Joseph, the man she'd met at the social. She could tell from his expression that he still felt uncomfortable among local people. He also hadn't gotten much sun yet. His pale skin almost blended with the aloha shirt he was wearing. Made of a fabric turned inside out, it had a small flower print. His high forehead wrinkled with worry as he negotiated the crowd leaving the church.

"Hi Joseph," she said, smiling.

"Hi Ellie," he said, relieved to see her. "How are you doing?"

"Well, not as good as I wish. Life has been difficult," she said, sighing.

"Oh no," he said as they walked down the steps. "What happened? Nothing serious, I hope."

"Just some family trouble—involving the computer. I caught the kids watching something they shouldn't have."

"You have teenagers?"

"Yes, Steven and Eric."

"Can't control it. It's in their DNA," Joseph said. "Or almost impossible to—unless you install one of those family-safe programs. A good one for Christians is Safe & Sure."

"Ah, really? I never heard of it. Is it expensive?"

"I think it costs $50 a year. You have to renew it yearly."

"That's kind of expensive."

"Less than $1 a week—worth it if you value peace of mind."

"Well, we can certainly use a good helping of that right now. Where are you off to? Going home?"

"I'm not sure. I thought I might do something different for a change. When you're retired and widowed, life can be the same day after day."

Ellie smiled sympathetically, trying to imagine what it would be like to be by herself. "Well, how about if I buy that program and you help me install it? Not really interesting, I know, but it would be a change."

"Sure, I have time today."

"Ted gets off from work at three. I'll surprise him."

"He works on Sunday?"

"He works security as a second job, and sometimes he has to fill in for other people. Today is just a regular shift."

"Has he been doing that for long?"

"Not too long. He doesn't get overtime work anymore—government cutbacks—so he had to find extra work."

"OK, well, I can swing by sometime after lunch. Around two? How does that sound?"

"Sure, that sounds great. We can have everything installed and working before Ted gets home."

"Tell me where you live." He pulled a pen and small notepad out of his breast pocket. She gave him her address and directions to the house.

When Ellie got home, she changed out of her dress and heels and into a short-sleeved blouse and bermuda shorts. At lunch, she explained to the boys that a church friend would be coming by to help her install a new computer program. Shortly after two, the doorbell rang and she answered it, then showed Joseph into the living room. The boys sat on the couch, watching TV.

"Eric and Steven, this is Joseph, a friend from church." Steven raised his hand and smiled shyly.

Eric looked the man over before greeting him. "Hey, Joseph."

"Boys, Joseph will be installing a new program on your computers—something that will help us keep track of things so that your dad and I don't have to keep checking on you. Should make things a lot easier."

The boys shared a glance. "Whatever," Eric said, then turned back to the TV.

Ellie led Joseph to the boys' room. The old gray tabby darted out as they approached. Joseph sniffed the air, pretending to smell something.

"Ah, my favorite cologne: Eau de Teenage Years." Ellie giggled. "Is the Internet connection on?"

"No, I have it turned off. Strict orders from Ted. Can't go on except for certain times of the day, and then one of us has to check on the boys every so often."

"A strict guy, your husband?"

"Well, yes, he likes to make rules—the more the better."

"But does he follow them?"

"Oh yes, he does. Next to the word *rule* in the dictionary is a picture of Ted—frowning, of course."

They laughed.

"He wasn't in the military, was he?"

"Air National Guard. For four years before we got married. I'll go turn on the Internet."

Joseph sat down at the computer, studying the boys' setup. The keyboard was dirty and sticky, dotted with soda and ketchup stains, and crumbs were lodged between the keys. The monitor had a few streaks of grease on it. Joseph turned on the computer, surprised to find only a guest account.

Ellie walked back in.

"Could I have something to wipe this keyboard with, Ellie? Looks like the boys haven't cleaned it recently."

"Of course. Be right back." She returned with a box of facial tissue.

"You don't have to log in to this computer? Has it always been that way?"

"The boys used to inherit Ted's old computers. The laptop over there is his. He keeps it in here in case one of them needs it. They finally got tired of his hand-me-downs and started looking around for an inexpensive one they could modify. Steven is quite good with computers. He used some savings to buy this from an online store and started building it up. Since Ted and the boys are the only ones who use it, I guess they felt they didn't need to log in."

"OK, but that does increase your vulnerability. Anyone can use the computer."

Ellie didn't reply, untroubled by the idea.

"Before we start, we might want to review the boys' browsing history— just to see if they've been visiting sites you want to know about." Joseph clicked a few times, and soon a list of URLs displayed on the screen.

Ellie pulled out the chair from the smaller desk and sat next to him. As he scrolled through the list, she scanned the items to see if anything stood out. She pointed to a line. "What's this?"

Joseph clicked on the link, and a new tab opened. In a few seconds, they were looking at a site called chatgirls.com. A woman wearing a red slip sat at a desk with a computer. The crude animation looped, showing her pulling her slip up over her thighs. In a corner of the page was a log-in field for account holders, and next to it was large green text: FOR ADULTS ONLY.

"Have you seen this site before?"

"No, never."

"Let's go back to the browsing history," Joseph said. He searched the list for "chatgirls" and found one more listing. "It looks like this site was visited twice in the last week."

"Did the boys create an account?"

"Well, we can try to find out." Joseph went to the browser's preferences and clicked on the privacy tab. "This is where we should be able to see what sites the boys created passwords for." He clicked again, and another window appeared. "Here is a list of sites that they created passwords for, and here, below, are sites they created unsaved passwords for."

"You mean they created passwords for these sites, but didn't save the passwords? Why would they do that?"

"Well, it usually indicates that someone wants to keep his access to a site secret."

Ellie and Joseph stared at the screen as he scrolled through the list of pages the boys had saved passwords for. In the list of unsaved passwords, there were only three lines: a log-in page, profile page, and mailbox—all for a site called Sexyfriends.com. Ellie watched as Joseph copied and pasted the URL into the address box. They were taken to another adult site: occupying most of the page was a picture of a large-breasted woman removing a bra top. Around it were smaller images of partly clad women.

Joseph returned to the browsing history and searched for "Sexyfriends." Finding nothing, he tried "sex." Pages for other sites came up, but none for Sexyfriends.com. He tried going further back, but the preferences were set to delete the browsing history after nine days.

"Well, it looks like someone created an account at Sexyfriends.com but hasn't looked at it recently. Either that, or he deleted the entry from the history."

"Can you do that?"

"Sure…Let's take a look at that laptop."

They moved their chairs to the smaller desk. The desk was old, cheaply made, and badly scuffed, as if it had been hauled through several homes.

Repeating the procedures, they found the same pages listed in the privacy pane of the browser on the laptop.

Ellie sighed deeply. "Oh, Lord…"

"You don't need to sit here. I can continue by myself."

"No, I want to. I want to find out what is going on."

"It looks like the only way to enter Sexyfriends is to create an account, so we have to stop."

"No—"

"No?"

"No, continue. Create an account."

Joseph clicked on the sign-up link and was taken to a form. Typing a few characters in each field, he clicked on the link to continue and was taken to a membership form. "Looks like you have to purchase a membership and enter your credit-card information before you can get an account. Either of the boys have a credit card?"

"Steven just got one."

"Well, if we had his statements, we could check to see if he purchased a membership here."

Ellie got up and started going through the file drawer in the bigger desk.

"Ellie, it might be better if we just ask Steven."

"No, no need. I know where almost everything is." Not finding what she was looking for, she walked over to one of the night tables. After pulling out the top drawer and then the bottom one, she clicked her tongue and said, "I found it."

The statements were in a used manila folder and dated back several months. There were only a few items listed for each month. Ellie commented as she scanned the statements. "Here is when he purchased the computer. And here's something: Xtreme Fun & Games. I wonder what that is."

Joseph opened a new tab, typed the words into the search field, and found it was the name of a game company. Ellie looked at the site and saw that it was where Steven had bought the game that upset her. She went back to the folder. "No...," she said as she finished looking at the last statement, "doesn't look like anything is here."

"Any way Eric could have bought a membership?"

"No, not unless he used someone else's credit card."

"Could he have used yours or Ted's?"

"I think Ted would have said something, and I don't think Eric used mine. I would have noticed. How much is the membership?"

"Basic level is $35 a month. I'm guessing it would be charged on the same day every month. So yeah, I'm sure you would have noticed something."

"My goodness: $35 a month? That's—what?—over $400 a year!"

"Ellie, is there any possibility Ted could have bought a membership?"

Her cheeks started to redden.

"Sorry, I didn't mean to upset you."

"No-no, you didn't. One day, we had a fight when I thought he had visited a porn site. When I confronted him, he got so angry—flew into a rage—that I thought I must be wrong, and I backed down."

"Do you think it might have meant something?"

"Yes, I'm worried," she said softly.

Joseph put his hand on her shoulder lightly. "It's OK...you have a right to feel what you feel. The Lord is revealing something to you—something that's hard to accept. Painful as it is, it's better to stand in the light of truth."

"Thank you, Joseph," Ellie said, starting to cry. She wiped her face with her hand, but her makeup ran and streaked her eyes and cheeks.

Joseph stood up and got the tissue box. He handed it to her, and she pulled out a few sheets. He looked away.

When Ted got home in the afternoon, Ellie and Joseph were sitting on the couch in the living room. He carried his helmet and gloves and had his backpack slung over his shoulder. Raising his hand to acknowledge them, he started to walk into the kitchen.

"Ted, this is Joseph," Ellie said, "a friend from church."

Ted walked back and said hello.

"Joseph helped me install a family-safe program called Safe & Sure. It costs $50 a year, but it will help us keep track of the boys."

"That's a lot. I wish you'd asked me first."

"Fifty dollars a year is a lot?" Ellie asked. "What about $35 a month?"

Ted froze. Ellie waited.

"What are you talking about, Ellie?"

"Thirty-five dollars a month is the cost of a basic membership at Sexyfriends.com. Isn't it, Ted? You get a profile page and your own mailbox."

Without saying another word, Ted turned and started up the stairs. Ellie ran after him and grasped his arm. He yanked it out of her grip.

"Ted, wait—"

He turned to look at her, and then at Joseph. Contempt filled his gaze. He started back up the stairs, meeting Eric on the landing.

"Dad—"

"Not now, son."

He strode rapidly to his room, gathered a few things, and stuffed them in his backpack. Then he walked back down.

Ellie stood at the foot of the stairs, blocking his way. She placed a hand on his chest and said, "Ted, stop. We need to talk."

"I have nothing to say. Get out of my way."

Joseph walked toward them. "We're not going to judge you—"

"Judge me—*judge me?!* You have no right to judge me or anyone else!"

Joseph halted.

"*Leave me alone!*" Ted yelled.

He strode out the door and to the garage, put on his helmet and gloves, and rode away. Turning right on Likelike Highway, he got on H-3 and headed west. He accelerated to fifty, then sixty. Within a minute, he was up to seventy, darting among the Sunday traffic.

Revolutions of guilt, shame, and anger passed through him, propelling him forward. He felt like a failure—the feeling was sharp and deep—yet he couldn't think of a defense or explanation. And what good did it do to explain or apologize anyway? He couldn't begin to say.

It was a clear day, but he saw only the images that streamed through his mind—fragments of memory, emotion-filled events—and heard nothing but the high-pitched, metallic sound of reproach: parents' friends' co-workers' his own. Clouds, sun, mountains, people sped past him, blended into a whole that somehow excluded him. He accelerated to eighty.

He was always getting into trouble as a child and being punished. Once, his mother beat him so hard with a broom that the handle broke. He told himself he would never cry again no matter how badly he was beaten. He would only be angry...In high school, he was chubby and quiet and felt different from the other kids. Deciding to go away, to leave the islands, he got into a small college on the mainland...Three years later, he learned about the Air National Guard and joined, attracted by the promise of new experiences. Finally he was able to become the kind of man he wanted to be: confident, strong, skilled. Learning how to parachute, use a gun, disarm bombs, he became one of the best men in the unit... In one of his college classes, he met a pretty girl. Ellie was three years younger and had light-brown hair, hazel eyes, and long legs. He didn't think she'd give him a second look, but one day she asked him to give her a ride on his motorcycle. They took off, and it felt good: her pressing against him, warm and close. When they got to some woods, she said she wanted to use the bathroom. He maneuvered the motorcycle into a clearing, and she walked off. He turned away. When he heard her walking back, he turned around and saw she had taken off her jeans. She walked up to him and stood close, taking his hand and putting it in her underwear. She was very wet. After that, they made love. Wanting her all the time, he thought it was the real thing...He graduated, finished his Guard service, and returned home. Living with his parents to save money, he got a job at a hospital. After Ellie graduated, he sent her money to come to Hawai'i, and they got married...Moving into their own apartment, they agreed he would be the breadwinner, but a year later she got a part-time job—the first of many times they'd agree on something and she would break her word. A few months after that, she started having an affair with Lane, a young guy she worked with. Soon she was making excuses about having to work extra hours. Three months later, Lane ended the affair, and brokenhearted, Ellie told Ted about it. He often thought of waiting at a certain bend in the road for Lane to drive by. He would have his gun ready... Then Ellie asked for forgiveness, and Ted forgave...Five years later, she was pregnant with Gwen, and then Steven and Eric came along. Ted insisted they attend church, and he was able to get part-time work there as a bookkeeper and groundskeeper. He turned his attention and energies to his family. In return for their faith, he thought, they would be favored. That was how life worked: you gave your heart to the Lord and tried to follow his teachings; then you had kids, and the Lord sheltered all of you and provided from his bounty...However, it didn't go that way, and Ted thought, Well, this is a test. I will succeed. I will regain the Lord's favor. But that never happened. A small step forward, a bit of progress, and then a big setback. Can a man be cursed by God? First, Ellie betrayed him, and then she was attacked and he was fired from the church. It was like being burned alive: unjustly accused, punished, then driven away. Not a single person stood by him. Again he resolved to not cry, to only be angry.

Ted kept riding, then turned onto H-1 in Halawa and got off the freeway to stop in Waipahu. He went to a small store to get a soda. Holding the bottle, he caught his reflection in the store window. An ordinary man. A wannabe hero. A hypocrite. A father who knelt in church and begged God to comfort his child. A husband who trolled sex sites for women. He was as weak as anyone: nothing special about him. He had no special strength to resist temptation. Theology, religious practice, principles: they were easily set aside. And just as easily returned to once the appetite for the flesh was sated.

He got back on the bike, deciding to drive up the west side of the island. The Hawai'i he remembered growing up in was still there: two-lane roads bounded not by sidewalks but by gravel-covered, leaf-strewn paths; low buildings that let the sun do its work and dazzle the eye.

Rounding a curve, he saw wind turbines on a ridge high above the road: pillars of white metal over a hundred feet tall, their blades turning like the spokes of a steamboat. Not of nature, not even of man, these sentinels seemed to receive their energy from a point beyond the sky. He was like them: set down on the earth for no purpose he could fathom. At one time, he had thought it was to be a good husband and father, to help lead a small community. But he discovered that was not to be his destiny. He was a man unlike other men, chained to the earth and belonging nowhere.

Regret and fatigue chased him as he wondered where he would stay till morning. The oranges and golds of dusk turned to shades of gray as Ted drove on, hoping to find a place dark enough to conceal himself.

case notes

Ted Koga appears defensive about the conflict between his religion and his sexual behavior, saying that no one but God has the right to judge him. At the same time, he recognizes that his behavior has gotten him into the predicament he's in: criminal investigation and possible dismissal from his job. We talked about the relationship between his wife's promiscuity and her grooming of their daughter: teaching Gwen how to behave around males and get them to cater to her needs and wants. He mentioned the entanglement of Ellie's needs and wants with Gwen's: how Ellie would oftentimes attempt to get Gwen's boyfriends to buy her things, include her when they went out on dates, etc. He said Gwen stopped bringing her boyfriends home because they felt uncomfortable. I asked if he had considered counseling and he said they had tried it when their daughter was assaulted, but Ellie had developed a hostile relationship with the therapist and brought the family sessions to a halt. I asked if he'd considered separating from her, and he replied with sarcasm, "Better the devil I know than the one I don't."

TK's wife has discovered his membership in the sex site. This came about when she and a male friend from church were installing a tracking program on the computers used by their sons, Steven and Eric. (This is related to the wife's discovery of the boys' sex-and-violence computer games.) TK came home from his second job and was confronted by his wife with the friend present. TK says that she "taunted" him. He became very angry, left the home, and has not returned. I asked him if his sons overheard the conversation, and he said he believes so. We discussed his staying elsewhere until he and wife can resolve this calmly. He said he has a few options: staying with his parents or one of his brothers. He said the latter was unlikely, but he could approach his younger brother Raymond as a last resort.

TK is staying temporarily with his parents. They are very concerned about the situation, though he has told them only that he and Ellie had a bad argument that compelled him to leave. He also told me the following: the parents are trying to allow him to resolve things by himself; he cannot continue to impose on them or return to his wife; he is reluctant to approach his brother; and a co-worker mentioned needing a live-in caretaker and handyman. Apparently, Ted and Raymond have a long-running rivalry that was exacerbated by Ellie's confiding in her brother-in-law about her marital problems.

TK has arranged to move into his co-worker's home. They will try this arrangement for a month. He has notified Ellie he is moving out, and he said she became upset and angry, insisting that he was deserting the family and abandoning his responsibilities. He said he told her that given the disclosures about his Internet activity, he could not be an effective husband or father and there was no point in remaining in the home. When she responded that Steven and Eric need a father to guide them into adulthood, he replied that he would continue to be there for them but not under the same roof. Ellie then brought up their bills and debts, and he said he would pay them, as always. About ten years ago, he had amassed a large debt and had had to file for bankruptcy; he thinks that she fears a repeat situation. She then asked if there was anything else he was doing that she should know about, and he replied it was none of her business. She threatened to tell his parents what was going on, and he yelled at her, insisting they keep this between the two of them.

TK asked me what I will say in my report to the base commander. I replied that as of today I believe he is fit to work but that he should continue with counseling after our sessions are over. He asked me for my evaluation, and I replied that his behavior deviates from the norm in significant respects and that he needs further counseling in order to resolve the underlying issues that cause him to seek gratification in deviant ways. He asked me to enumerate the issues, and I replied that there appear to be four main ones: (1) alienation from his own needs and wants; (2) merging of feelings of sexual rejection with deep shame and anger; (3) lack of a normal, fulfilling relationship with a woman; and (4) compensating desire to control and dominate people, in particular women. I added that in describing his home, he portrayed a charged environment in which the boundaries of healthy, appropriate behavior were frequently being crossed.

TK continued our previous discussion, saying that he was angry I would say he desired to dominate women. As contrary evidence, he recounted several incidents involving his wife, daughter, and mother, and I replied that control and domination occur in very specific ways: through his use of pornography and his initiation of random sexual contact with strangers at adult sites. These kinds of experiences create the illusion of complete control for men like him, and it is this illusion that is at the core of the addictive experience. When he asked what I meant by "men like him," I said men who attempt to get women to respond to them with the frequency and intensity they equate with female submission to masculine power. He said he is not like that, and I pulled out the form about sexual fantasies and said his answers indicate that, for him, female surrender and incapacitation of will are components of sexual gratification. He stopped speaking, and we ended the session in silence. At the end, he stood up and left.

Ellie has told TK that she would excuse his behavior if he would return to the home and receive counseling from their pastor. When I asked him if he'd consider that, he said no. He said he doesn't respect the pastor and, in any case, is unable to keep his marriage vows. He recognizes the contradiction between his religious beliefs and his behavior, but wants to keep things in suspension, thinking he will do the least harm that way. I asked about the effect of the separation on Steven and Eric, and he replied that he has not spoken to his sons since leaving the home. However, he said, Ellie has told him that Eric is starting to act out at school and that this may lead to problems.

I explained to TK that the questionnaires he filled out provided baseline data and that I now need to collect more information to chart his progress. When I asked him if he had viewed pornographic material since we started the sessions, he replied that he had tried to do so at an Internet cafe, but circumstances prevented him from continuing. I asked him what kind of material he had tried to view, and he said it was a sex video. I asked him why he didn't bring this up when it happened, and he said he felt it was a minor event as the attempt had been aborted. I informed him that I would have to include this information in my report. He became angry. I explained that it was a matter of disclosure: he had not reported the incident at the time it had occurred, and in effect, he was making a decision for me and others. That was information the base commander would want to have.

TK says Eric is beginning to have problems at school and threatened to hit a schoolmate who'd been bullying him. TK says he was called to the school and had to meet with the counselor, teacher, and principal. I asked about Ellie, and he said that she was unable to make the meeting because of her job. He works the second shift at the military base, and because the incident happened in the morning, he was able to meet with the school staff. They agreed that the boy will begin weekly sessions with the counselor. Ted will receive reports and speak with the counselor by phone when necessary.

TK asked if I was still going to recommend that he continue therapy, and I said yes. He then asked if I could be the therapist he should continue with, and I replied that there were many people who could help him. He said that it was mainly a matter of convenience for him: not only was I on base, but I also had all his information and he would not have to repeat himself or get to know someone new. I explained that our sessions had been arranged in response to a request from the base commander and that we could not continue the arrangement. He asked if I had a private practice, and I said yes. He then asked if he could see me as a private patient. I replied that he should think about that option and try to make an objective decision. If he concluded our sessions were beneficial, I would accept him as a new patient. He seemed relieved and said I was not a bad person even though my thinking had been corrupted by my training and my liberal bias. He then said he's concluded I have to disagree with him often in order to keep my own views firm and intact. I refrained from smiling.

⅗

REPORT TO BASE COMMANDER (DRAFT FOR REVIEW AND COMMENT)

SUMMARY

Civilian employee Ted Koga is being investigated in relation to the assault and attempted murder of Ginger Wong. Mr. Koga contacted Ms. Wong on his own electronic device and on his own time. His off-site activities led to his implication in the crime and, eventually, the involvement of this base. As requested, I have met with Mr. Koga three times a week for the last four weeks in order to determine his fitness to continue working here, and have prepared this report of my findings and recommendations.

COMMENTS

Mr. Koga's consumption of pornography began as casual browsing and escalated to active membership in an adult site and daily trolling for sex partners. This is how he came in contact with Ms. Wong and jeopardized himself. Since meeting with federal investigators, he has terminated his membership in the adult site and attempted to refrain from visiting other such sites. He seems cognizant of the errors that led to his being investigated. However, upon further questioning by me, he revealed that he subsequently tried to view a pornographic video. When I asked why he did not inform me of the incident when it happened, he said that he felt it was not important because the attempt had been aborted. I replied that he was in effect making a decision about what I and others should know about his activities, and this was a violation of our agreement to cooperate for his and the base's benefit.

I have determined that Mr. Koga was disposed to escalating use of pornography because of (1) the illusion of anonymity and privacy on the Internet and (2) such factors as the following: shaming and humiliation by his wife; anger at her betrayal of her marriage vows; anger at betrayal by his church (he was falsely accused by a church member and then released from a part-time position with the organization); financial problems, compelling him to work two jobs; alienation from his own needs and wants; and impulsive, risk-taking behavior.

As we know, the use of pornography by federal employees has risen sharply over the last decade and is now responsible not only for the compromise of federal information systems but also for increased security threats. I have determined that Mr. Koga is fit to continue working without change to his security clearance, but I recommend that base command take reasonable and adequate measures to insure the integrity of this base.

RECOMMENDATIONS

1. Mr. Koga should be monitored for the entirety of his federal employment. We can't predict when circumstances will conspire to create optimum conditions for recurrence of his risk-taking behavior and when such behavior might endanger the security of this base. The Employee Assistance Program can work with Human Resources on how to carry out this monitoring.

2. While acknowledging that Mr. Koga is responsible for his actions, we can help reduce the financial pressure on him. I recommend that base command allow him to resume performing overtime and emergency work.

3. Mr. Koga should continue seeing a therapist to work on anger management, financial problems, risk-taking behavior, and the trauma of shame, humiliation, and betrayal.

cc: Human Resources
     FBI

part ii

After discovering one's real self, it is difficult to live.

INTIZAR HUSAIN

waif

Ted rode his motorcycle into the wooden, two-car garage on Sierra Drive. It was late Sunday afternoon, and Lester Ogata, his co-worker and friend, was working on his Toyota Camry. An hour before, Ted had gotten off from his second job, then decided to stop at the supermarket.

As he was coming up the hill, he had felt his cell phone buzzing in the breast pocket of his jacket. He took the phone out and flipped it open, but didn't recognize the number. He never responded unless he knew the number. He put the phone away.

The car hood was up, and Les was cussing and shaking his head. "Suckin' guys!"

"Hey, Les. Trouble with the Camry?"

"Dis bugga need new plugs and I just wen replace 'em last year!"

"You need one motorcycle," Ted teased.

"Me? I too fat for ride one motorcycle! I fall off, I goin' make one giant pothole!" They laughed.

Les was a good worker at the military base, and though twelve years younger than Ted, he never competed with him. Sometimes the younger guys would ride Ted, trying to show him up or provoke him into getting angry. Les got along well with Ted, content to follow the lead of an older, more experienced man.

"Check you later," Ted said.

"Shuah ting, brah."

Ted walked down the narrow concrete steps, bounded by white torch ginger, to the lower level. The house had been built in the sixties, and Les had tried to help his father, an insurance executive, keep it up. But Mr. Ogata had died the year before, and the burden of grief—his mother's and his own—had made it all too much for him. Grateful to have a place to stay, Ted kept the grass watered and mowed, the mango and plumeria trees pruned, and the mock-orange hedge trimmed. He had also worked on the toolshed, patching and treating the wood walls, putting in a new vinyl floor, and painting the corrugated tin roof. Looking at the wall Mr. Ogata had built specially for the tools, Ted thought that he would have liked the man. Tools for similar tasks were grouped together, and the pegs and hooks were carefully spaced to allow organization of items large and small. Floor-to-ceiling shelves accommodated supplies, bins, and containers of various shapes and sizes.

Ted thought of repairs as challenges to his manhood and prided himself on coming up with solutions to the problems that plagued the old house. Les would fume and cuss, and Ted would chide his friend, then suggest what to do. He also tried to be economical, recommending they spend as little as possible. Here, Les challenged his friend, insisting that they not skimp. He had few expenses other than the home, so he wanted to buy the best materials he could afford. He owed it to his parents, he told Ted.

Ted unlocked the door and walked to the kitchen table, slipping off the army-surplus backpack. He removed his silver helmet, black jacket and gloves, and unzipped the backpack, taking out two bags of groceries. He checked the eggs to make sure none had cracked, and put away the carton, packs of hot dogs, bag of chips, and liter of soda. Then he sat down and looked at his phone again. Whoever had called had left a message.

"Dad, I'm in trouble. I need your help. I'm at a gas station by a school...Kawā-nanakoa. Please...help me..."

Ted jumped up, his heart starting to pound. He grabbed his helmet, jacket, and gloves and rushed out, slamming the door and running up the steps. "Les, you know where Kawānanakoa School is?"

"Yeah, da intermediate school by da kine...Liliha Bakery. You know, Nuʻuanu side. Eh, someting wrong, Ted? You look mad."

"I need to go help my daughter. I'll be back soon." Ted tried to keep his voice under control.

"She in trouble?"

"Cannot tell, but no worry. I got it covered."

"Eh, take da Vineyard exit, but be careful. Got police at da bottom of da hill."

"OK, gotcha. Thanks."

Ted got on the bike, strapping on his helmet and pulling down the visor. He rode back down the hill, taking care not to speed, though adrenalin was coursing through his body. Getting onto the H-1 on-ramp by the gas station, he merged with the cars heading west.

As he got closer to town, the traffic increased. To handle the load, the state transportation department had narrowed the lanes and added one. He noted a freeway sign: MOTORCYCLES USE EXTREME CAUTION.

Minutes later, he came to the off-ramp for Vineyard Boulevard and took the exit, slowing to thirty. He drove up Vineyard, then turned onto Nuʻuanu Avenue. There was a 7-Eleven a few blocks down the road. He slowed as he passed, scanning the place in case Gwen was there. Not seeing her, he continued, driving past the school. Across the street was a Chevron station. He saw someone sitting hunched over at the far end. Branches from a large tree cast a shadow on Gwen.

Ted brought the bike to a stop alongside her, then took his helmet off and put it on the seat.

"Gwen...Gwen!" She didn't look up. He knelt in front of her, took his gloves off, and put his hand under her chin to raise her head. Her skin was cold, and her eyes were half-closed. He gently lifted the lids. Her eyes were glazed over. Her hair and clothes were dirty, and she smelled of urine.

He stood up, got out his phone, and called information for the number of a taxi company. The number rang, and he waited for a dispatcher to answer. "Yeah, can you send a cab right away to the Chevron station across from Kawānanakoa Intermediate on Nuʻuanu? Yeah, thanks."

He slipped the phone back in his pocket and knelt again. "Gwen... Gwen...I've called a taxi. I'm taking you home with me." She didn't respond.

Shortly afterward, a white minivan pulled into the station, and Ted waved at it. The cab approached him and Gwen, then stopped. Ted walked over to the driver's side and said, "I want you to take this young woman to Sierra Drive in Kaimukī." The driver got out slowly and walked over to Gwen.

He seemed worried. "I don't know. Maybe she should go hospital? Kuakini right over there," he said, pointing with his left hand.

"No!" Ted said, surprising himself by raising his voice. "I mean no, please do as I asked. Let's get her into your car."

"She smells bad, and she's dirty."

"Yeah. Here," Ted said, handing the driver his jacket, "put this on your seat."

"You sure?" the driver asked, looking at the jacket. Ted nodded. The driver walked back to the cab.

Ted bent down and put his hands under Gwen's arms, lifting her up. Then he put one arm around her waist and half walked, half carried her to the cab. The driver slid the door open, and Ted lifted her onto the seat.

"I'll meet you guys there. Got that?"

The driver looked even more worried. Ted finally realized why.

"It's OK," he said. "I'm her dad."

The cab drove away, and Ted got back on his motorcycle. He rode down Nuʻuanu Avenue, then turned left onto Vineyard Boulevard, staying in the left lane to get on the freeway. Twenty minutes later, he pulled into the Sierra Drive garage. Les was gone, and the cab hadn't arrived. Ted ran down the concrete steps, unlocked the door, and propped it open. Moving quickly, he pulled his folding mattress out, threw it on the floor, and grabbed a sheet and blanket. Then he went to the bathroom, pushed the curtain aside, and ran the water to fill the tub. He heard the cab pull up and park.

He ran back up, paid the driver, and lifted Gwen out of the cab. As he started to walk away, the driver said, "Eh, your jacket." "Oh yeah, thanks," Ted replied as the man laid it across Gwen.

Walking carefully as he carried her, Ted turned sideways to avoid hitting the ginger plants next to the steps. The concrete was cracked in a few places, so he moved slowly and deliberately. He brought her into the house, rested her on the floor, then took his shoes off. Putting the sheet and blanket on the folding mattress, he glanced at her. She hadn't moved. He carried her into the bathroom and set her down, laying his jacket on the side. When he started to remove her clothes, he discovered that she was wearing more than one layer: underneath the long-sleeved sweatshirt were two T-shirts, and underneath the jeans was a pair of capris, but she had no underwear. He checked the pockets, finding two dollars and a few coins. The clothes were soiled, and he threw them in a corner. She looked like she'd lost twenty pounds since she lived at home, and she had a black, barbed-wire tattoo around her waist. Her middle name, Hanako, was tattooed on the front of her right shoulder. Track lines went down her arms. He lifted her and put her in the bathtub, squeezing his shampoo bottle into the running water. Then he got a towel, rolled it up, and put it under her head and shoulders. All the while, her eyes were closed. He knelt by the tub and leaned back on his heels, letting out a deep breath.

What a beautiful girl she had once been, and smart too, he recalled as he studied her face. Hapa-haole, she had light-brown hair and eyes, long lashes, and a model's high cheekbones and pretty mouth. He'd been so proud of her as she made As in school, but her mother's influence soon messed up his dreams for her success. Ellie taught her how to dress, wear makeup, and behave around boys. Gwen had them following her around as soon as she hit her teens. She had nearly failed to graduate from high school, too distracted by the attention of boys and the efforts of jealous girls to make her look bad. A self-destructive streak ran through her too, and she had crashed two cars by the time she was twenty. Ted had given up trying to be a good influence on her, though he would respond when she talked about her future.

He moved strands of hair off her face and reflected on how life had shaped those bones and muscles into something hard and cold—something that courted the bad in people. He thought about the time he had seen her at the Pali. He had tried to hug her then, glad to see her and glad to not have hurt himself worse in the accident. But she had resisted his touch, and he had not tried again.

He stood and gazed at himself in the mirror: graying hair; eyes filled with resignation. He walked into the living room, lay down on the couch to rest, and was asleep in a few minutes.

Awhile later, Gwen opened her eyes. She couldn't figure out where she was and how she'd gotten there, but she knew her father was somewhere nearby. She felt the rolled towel behind her head and grabbed it, bringing it in front of her face, then put it on the floor. Though weak, she tried to bathe and to wash her hair. Then she picked up the towel, stood, and put it around herself. She peeked into the living room and saw Ted sleeping on the couch. She stepped back and went into the bedroom. Going through his clothes, she tried to find something she could wear. She found a brown T-shirt and navy-blue shorts. They were so big she stuffed the shirt in the shorts and rolled the waist down. Tentatively, she walked into the living room and lay down on the folding mattress, pulling the blanket over her. She was somewhere safe, she knew. Turning on her side to face her father, she rested her cheek on her palm and smelled the clean sheet and blanket. And then she closed her eyes and smiled the smile of a little girl.

Ted awoke to Gwen's groaning. He looked at his watch: almost nine. In the moonlight coming through the picture window, he saw her rolling on the mattress, clutching her stomach. He turned on the lamp, and she tried to get up. He put his arms around her waist and lifted her so that she could stand. She was breathing hard, and drops of sweat fell from her face. "Bathroom..."

"Do you have to go?"

She nodded vigorously.

He helped her there. She knelt before the toilet, clutched the seat with both hands, and started to heave. Liquid fell from her mouth into the bowl. She groaned, crying. She continued to heave, but only a pale-green liquid fell. She tried to speak. "I hurt..."

"Do you want to go to the hospital, Gwen? We can go right now."

Her eyes widened. *"No, never!"* she screamed.

"Gwen, you have no food in your stomach. You're throwing up stomach acids and juices. That's why it hurts."

"I'm not going!" Tears mingled with sweat on her face.

Ted grabbed a face towel and wet it in the sink. She collapsed on the floor, rolling into a ball. He walked into the kitchen with the towel, got a pitcher out of the fridge, poured ice water on the towel, and wrung it.

His cell phone rang.

"Um, sorry, Ted, but everyting OK? Mom—she wen wake up. Can hear your daughter. She sick or what? Maybe she should go hospital? What you tink? I can drive, braddah, no problem."

"Thank you, Les. Very nice of you to offer, but Gwen hates hospitals—long story. I'm gonna try and feed her something she can keep down. Sorry for the noise. Please tell your mom I said sorry."

"'Course, braddah. But you call, 'kay, if need help. I right here."

"Sure. Thank you, Les. You're a good man."

"You too, braddah."

Ted went back to the bathroom, knelt down, slipped his hand under Gwen's head, and wiped her face. "Hon, we need to get some food in you. Can you understand me?"

She didn't respond. He stood, got a bath towel, and put it on her to keep her warm.

"Gwen, I'm going to make some food for you, OK? I'll be right back." Ted went into the kitchen and opened the pantry: white bread, peanut butter, jam, packets of seasoning, a fifteen-pound bag of rice, meals-ready-to-eat he'd picked up at the base, potato chips, soda. Then he remembered the boxes of instant saimin on top of the fridge. He grabbed a bag, tore it open, and sprinkled some of the powder into a saucepan. After filling it with water, he turned the heat on and broke the cake of dry noodles in two. When the broth started to boil, he put half the noodles in. He started to stir when he saw them loosening. It was too hot for Gwen, he realized, so he turned off the heat. He found a large bowl and stirred the noodles some more. Then he poured the saimin in the bowl, got a glass of ice water, and grabbed some plastic utensils.

He raised her up, propping her on his lap, and tried to feed her. He scooped a spoonful of broth, blew on it to cool it, and poured it into her mouth. She swallowed, tasting with her tongue the liquid on her lips. Using a fork, he tried to give her a few noodles. She chewed them, swallowed, and coughed. He picked up the glass and tipped it against her mouth so that she could drink. She kept it down. He waited a few minutes, then gave her more. For half an hour, he fed her.

Her eyes started to flutter and close. He put the bowl down and, careful not to knock anything over, slid his arms under her, carried her to the mattress, and set her down. He retrieved the bowl and glass and put them in the sink with the saucepan. Then he closed the curtains and turned off the lamp. It was after ten.

In the bathroom, he wiped the floor where Gwen's tears and sweat had fallen. Then he took a shower, the cold water hitting his chest like a hard punch and making him cough.

Minutes later, he walked into the dark bedroom and lay down, falling asleep as soon as he closed his eyes.

voices

"Sweetheart...Gwen..." Bending at the waist, Ted stood over Gwen as she lay on the floor. "I need to leave for work now. This morning I went out and got some food for you: crackers, sugarless Jell-O, energy drinks, fruits. I cut up some apples and left them in the fridge. Your stomach is really raw, so don't eat the other things in the fridge, OK? If the energy drinks are too strong, water them down or add ice cubes. You need to replace the fluids you lost. Got all that?"

She smiled weakly.

"And brush your teeth. Can't have my girl walking around without teeth."

She laughed softly and nodded her head.

"I left the number of the base operator on the table. Call if there's an emergency, and they'll reach me. Remember that I work the second shift, so I'll be home late, around eleven." Ted knelt to kiss her forehead, then stood up, grabbed his things off the table, and walked out the door.

Gwen looked at the sky through the picture window. She felt empty, as if she'd been held upside down by the ankles until her feelings and thoughts had drained out of her. She'd had a nightmare, the same one she'd been having for years. A man lay on top of her, holding her down. No matter how hard she tried, she couldn't get him off, couldn't call for help.

She wrapped the blanket around herself tightly and closed her eyes.

The sun shone through the window, but Gwen shivered. She turned over and, grasping the couch, tried to stand. Shakily, she walked to the bedroom, looking for something more to cover herself with. Except for a sheet and pillow, her father's bed was bare, and she remembered that he often slept without a blanket. She walked to the closet, thinking she might find a jacket. She went through his clothes, pushing aside one thing after another, then came to a group of empty metal hangers. Grabbing them to push them aside, she found them surprisingly cold. As she held them, they lost their hardness, then bent and conformed to her hand, gripping her fingers. She heard voices. Starting as rustling sounds, they became whispers, first soft and then loud. She stepped back, dazed and frightened.

She stumbled to the bathroom and pulled a bath towel off the rack, then saw her reflection in the mirror: an old woman with ragged skin and drooping eyes and cheeks. She had lost some of her hair, and the rest stuck out as if she'd been standing in a gale. Clutching the towel, she rushed back to her bed, crying and trembling.

When Ted came home, he saw that the living room was dark. The light in the bathroom was on.

"Gwen?"

"I'm in here, Dad."

He sighed, thankful she was all right. "What are you doing?"

"Trying to find another toothbrush. You know you only have one good one?"

He walked to the kitchen table, slipped off his things, and sat down to take off his shoes. "We'll get you a good one tomorrow. Promise."

Gwen came out, walking slowly. "How was your day?"

"How was *your* day?"

"Rough, awful," she said, sitting down carefully on the couch. "I started hallucinating."

"Oh no!"

"Yeah, I was so scared I cried myself to sleep. When I got up, I thought of Grandma. I looked up her number in the phone book and called her."

"And?"

"And she asked me where I was, how I got here. I couldn't say much except that I was with you and you were taking care of me. She sounded relieved. Then I told her about my hallucination. I went to the closet and saw the hangers come alive, Dad. They started to bend and touch me, hold my fingers. Then I heard voices. Grandma asked me if I was on drugs, and I said no. She said, 'Are you sure?' and I said I was before. She told me not to be scared, because she loves me and you love me. Then she said she had worried about me since I was a baby. I said I loved her too. I told her I had run away from my boyfriend and was living on the street, but you saved me. It sounded like she was laughing, but I think she was crying. She told me to tell you to bring me over there sometime."

Ted sighed again, angry at himself for not being with Gwen when she needed help. "Hon, why don't you take my bedroom? I can sleep out here."

"No, Dad."

"Why not?"

"It's too dark in your room, and your things are in there. Ghosts live in there. I want to stay out here, in the living room. I can see the sky and the clouds. And besides, it's closer to the food." She smiled.

"OK. But what should we do if you hallucinate tomorrow?"

"Do you have a radio? Maybe you can leave it on, and I can listen to music or the news. If something can drown out the voices in my head..."

Ted stared at her, concerned. "Hon, if you hear the voices tomorrow, we need to take you to a doctor."

"No, no doctor."

"Gwen—"

"I said no doctor!"

Ted shook his head.

"Hon, I talked to Les about the situation. He's taking today off. If anything happens and you feel scared, just call upstairs. The number is on the table."

"Who's Les?"

"Lester Ogata. He and his mom own this house. They're letting me stay here for now."

"Did you leave Mom?"

"Yes."

"Why?"

"I'll explain everything soon, OK? Got to get to work early—special project coming up. I bought grapes—they're in the fridge—and a toothbrush. You be good—no poking around in people's closets, OK?" He pointed to the end table. "There's my clock radio. You turn it on when you feel like."

"Dad, I don't know if I'll call Les. I don't know him."

"He's a good guy. I work with him at the base."

"And he knows who I am?"

"He knows *about* you—enough to help if you need it." Ted leaned over and kissed her on the forehead.

A headache wracked Gwen. She tried to stand but fell back down on the mattress. The pounding made her clutch her head. She remembered the energy drinks and tried again to stand. She took a few steps, her head splitting, then a few more and reached the fridge. She opened the door: there were six bottles, two each of grape, orange, and lemon flavors. She grabbed the grape drink, twisted off the cap, and drank. The cold liquid made her head pound harder. She put the cap back on and looked for the grapes. Taking a bunch to the sink, she washed them and then got in bed. Lying on her back, she rested the grapes on her chest and started to eat. Involuntary tears came, triggered by her headache, and she opened her mouth wide, trying to breathe and eat while crying. Tears flowed down her neck and onto her hair.

Weakly, she stood up again and, leaning against the walls, made her way to the bathroom. She opened the medicine cabinet and found a big bottle of aspirin, remembering that her father took it frequently for his aches and pains. She put two tablets in her mouth, bent over the sink, and drank from the faucet. Her head started to spin, and she clutched the countertop.

*I hurt…I hurt…I hurt…*She lay down on the cool bathroom floor and closed her eyes.

"Hon, Gwen…"

She awoke, surprised to see her father when it was still daylight.

"Are you OK?" She nodded. "I was able to come home early. Tomorrow I'll stay here." He helped her up, then back to bed. He shook out the blanket and laid it across her gently.

"I'm making something simple for dinner: chicken broth with rice. That should be OK on your stomach."

"Thank you, Dad."

The next day, Ted worked in the yard, mowing the grass, trimming the hedge, and fertilizing and watering the mango and plumeria trees. He paid special attention to the torch ginger and Japanese forest grass on the sides of the house. As he worked, he thought about what Mrs. Ogata had told him about her husband. Mr. Ogata had bought many of his yard tools from Japan, considering American ones inferior, and planted the gold forest grass and white torch ginger to beautify the property. He had regarded his home as one of the neighborhood gems.

Ted thought about his own home in Kāneʻohe. He had bought the house after the mortgagor had foreclosed on it. The former owners had not treated the house well, and it needed many repairs, as well as a paint job inside and out. Ted had tried to keep up the property but didn't have the time and money to do enough, and his own family was neglectful and irresponsible. By the time Gwen left, he was only doing repairs and replacing appliances when necessary.

Gwen sat on the couch, watching her father as he moved from one corner of the yard to another. Easy-listening music played on the radio, and she looked at the magazines he had borrowed from Mrs. Ogata. Sometimes he would disappear for a while, then reappear with a different tool in his hand. Every hour or so, he'd peer through the window to check on her, and she'd flash the victory sign.

Midafternoon, he came in, sweating. "Any voices? Weird hangers?"

"Nope, not today. I love this TV show," she said, pointing to the picture window and smiling.

"Dad, can you give me a piece of nice paper and an envelope? I want to write Grandma a letter."

"Sure, I have some in my night table. When you're done, I'll address the envelope for you."

"Thank you!"

It was now a week since Gwen had come to the Ogata home. She sat at the kitchen table, writing about the house, the view, the fragrant mock-orange hedge, and Lester and Mrs. Ogata. She ended by telling her grandmother, "This afternoon when Dad got home, I opened a package of saimin. I cooked it, added a raw egg, and set the table. Dad sat down to eat, and 'he saw that it was good.'"

After she signed the letter, she read it over and drew a smiling heart next to her signature.

sirens

Agent Johnson did most of the talking this time. "Ginger Wong worked for a group that was trying to create a large database on people here—both men and women who might be vulnerable for one reason or another and who could be exploited. She had several identities at Sexyfriends.com to maximize the number of hits she got and to collect as much data on her 'correspondents' as possible. Her group periodically purchased information on site members in Hawaiʻi and researched and profiled each one. That included you.

"Someone took your picture—it could have been taken anywhere, anytime—and it was added to your profile. A retirement party, birthday celebration, Boss's Day luncheon—maybe someone took your picture with his smartphone or tablet. Eventually, it was added to the picture taken at Pink & Drink—skillfully added. It wasn't until we went there that we learned you could not have been sitting where you were in relation to Ms. Wong and her group."

"But camera phones are prohibited at the base," Vince Reynaldo said.

"Prohibited maybe, but people carry them anyway, don't they? And certainly when they leave the base. Mr. Koga, you attended off-site functions, didn't you?"

"Rarely, but yeah, a few. Why come after me, though? I'm poor. I have two jobs, and I'm still barely making it."

"Barely making it makes you a good target for exploitation and manipulation. Besides which, money from people like you is just one kind of payoff. Suppose there exists another network, with more assets and a larger reach, that bought information from Wong's group."

"Still doesn't make sense. Nothing special about me."

"You work with defense equipment, don't you? You get into places most people never see, and you have a mechanic's understanding and knowledge of these areas—not only how they're designed but also their weaknesses, their problems. That information could potentially be useful to someone. It may not seem likely to you, but stranger things have happened."

"So somehow they connected me with my member identity?"

"Yes. Not only can buyers of lists get people's names and addresses but also some of their other information, including site identities. How much time you spent at Sexyfriends.com, how many women you wrote to, which women, how many times—it all gets recorded at the site. And sometimes that information gets into the hands of other people."

"So their so-called privacy policy is a sham?"

"When you signed up, did you read the membership terms carefully? Most people don't. There are clauses that cancel others or exempt the site owners in certain situations. In addition, you might not have opted out of certain kinds of marketing appeals."

Ted fell silent, thinking about the offers that came to him. He deleted almost all of them, but once in a while the subject line would make him pause and he'd read the message. He was careful not to click on any links, but occasionally he'd copy or type a URL into the address box. Sometimes he liked where he ended up; other times, he exited quickly.

"So these folks—they have a lot of information on me?"

"Their profile for you included your work history, financial history, property, family members, and so forth. A lot of this information can easily be found or purchased on the Internet. Once amassed into a profile, though—and added to your activities at Sexyfriends—it can create a picture of someone with quite a lot of vulnerability. When you wrote to Ms. Wong, a standard set of procedures kicked in and she was directed to contact you."

"So it wasn't about…?"

"Sex? No, for the guys on the other end, sex is just a means of luring their targets. Once she established a relationship with you, her goal was to compromise you."

"That's why she was attacked?"

"Well, that is one of our theories." Johnson smiled.

"So what? Am I still a suspect?"

"In relation to the attack on Ginger Wong, you are no longer a suspect. However, your file is still open. And information could be added to it at any time."

Ted looked at the manila folder sitting on the table. "I don't understand. Why is it still open?"

"Dr. Ho'okano recommended that you be monitored for the duration of your employment by the base. We are keeping your file open in case we need to add to it at some point."

"What? When did she do that?"

"In her report to the base commander."

"Is the report in that folder?"

"Yes."

"Can I see it?"

"No."

"I can't see a report that's about me and affects me?"

"Dr. Ho'okano's report is an internal document prepared for the base commander. If you wish to see it, you can make an appointment with Human Resources. Dr. Ho'okano cc'd them, so your personnel file probably has a copy. Be aware that someone has to monitor your examination of the file."

"What?!"

"Ted," Vince said, "your personnel file is government property. Someone has to make sure you don't alter, deface, or tamper with it."

Ted dropped his head back and made a fist.

Agent Park spoke. "Mr. Koga, did you share confidential information about any aspect of your job with family members or friends?"

Ted unclenched his fist slowly, aware that Vince was listening more closely. "Well, no..."

"Did you talk to anyone about your job?"

"My family."

"Anyone else?"

"Well..." Ted grimaced. "I had a girlfriend..."

Vince rolled his eyes and said, "A *girlfriend?* Wow, you really get around, huh?"

Ted didn't reply.

"What is your girlfriend's name and occupation?"

"My ex-girlfriend. We broke up some months back. Her name is Claudia Wilkins. She's a speech therapist."

"How did you meet her?"

Ted looked down. "At a dating site."

"Did you share confidential information about your job with her?"

"No. I...would talk about problems I was having with the guys or delays in our work—general stuff like that. Nothing specific."

"Nothing that would compromise the security of this base?"

"No, nothing."

"Well, Mr. Koga," Johnson said, "if you remember anything, please do contact us. Also, remember that withholding information could make things worse for you. We don't want that to happen, do we now?" Johnson smiled again.

⚡

In an announcement affecting users in five countries, Eros Unlimited (EU) confirmed that its most popular site, Sexyfriends.com, was the target of a data sweep at 3 a.m. ET yesterday. Personal information on the site's four million users was stolen by a group identifying itself as Rightfield.

EU, parent company of the site, operates a mail-order business for adult toys as well as two other adult sites. CEO and founder Dwight McCall accused Rightfield of violating "the privacy of millions of innocent men and women" and said EU was cooperating fully with law enforcement agencies in the US and elsewhere.

In a statement released to the media, Rightfield said it was "lashing back at the tens of thousands of human traffickers, perverts, and sociopaths who make up Sexyfriends.com's audience." The group said that unless the site was taken down, it would start releasing data in batches of 100 users, beginning with the "hypocrites that belong to religious organizations and police agencies."

Visitors to the site are informed that it is "down for maintenance until further notice." McCall insists that the site will be back up and that Rightfield "will suffer the full force of the law."

As Ted read the news article, he tried to calculate the effect of this development. Was his information at Sexyfriends.com part of the data sweep even though he was no longer a member? He reflected on the news that had been announced that morning at the military base: the Chinese had hacked into federal government servers and stolen the personal data of twenty-three million employees, including their medical records. On both lists, would he be doubly jeopardized? But there had to be hundreds of people like him—thousands even. He wouldn't stand out. He would simply blend in, a gray shadow blending into other shadows. Not a man, just a gray shape against a gray background: a faceless, nameless, flat figure. *We all chose the same thing, thinking we were doing it anonymously, protected by privacy and security measures.*

Ted hung his head and looked down at his feet, thinking about where they'd led him. But perhaps he'd done the leading, humiliated by his wife, tempted by the ads and images that appeared on the edges of his computer screen. Now that pornography had entered the mainstream, little was withheld, banned, forbidden. More and more—and younger as time went by—actresses, models, singers, celebrities showed more of themselves. Breasts, nipples, thighs, stomachs, hips, buttocks...

Toward midnight, Ted checked his email, surprised to see a message from Ellie. The subject line read ELDER MORI, and the message contained just a link. He clicked on it and was taken to the Police Beat section of the newspaper. He scanned the items, reading the third one carefully.

Police responding to a call last night found Satoshi Mori, 83, slumped over his desk at the Wahiawa Salvation Church. Mori was the subject of two sexual harassment lawsuits filed recently and settled out of court. A custodian found the body. The police have ruled out foul play.

the cut

At the shopping mall, Ted sat in a chair and read a magazine while Gwen got her hair cut. He came across an article on paragliding, looked at the pictures of men and women, and read their praise of the sport. He'd wanted to return to the air for decades. *Maybe this is the way to do it...Expensive, though.*

"Hey, Dad, what do you think?" Gwen faced him, then turned around. Gone was nearly a foot of hair. The hairdresser had given her bangs that sloped across her forehead from left to right and had cut the hair by her ears close to her head. The hair in back was cut straight across and skimmed the base of her neck.

"Wow, cute!" Ted said. He closed the magazine and put it aside.

Gwen giggled, and Ted was surprised to discover how glad he was to see her long hair gone. She'd worn it in such a way as to attract attention, and he realized it had bothered him when boys and men turned their heads to look.

"Dad," she said as he was paying, "can we go to a drugstore next?"

"Why? What do you need there?"

"Well, remember I used to wear contacts? I lost them a long time ago, and I was wondering if I could maybe try those cheap glasses they have on the racks."

"Yeah, you can try it, I guess."

Ted marveled at how the new haircut made Gwen seem like a different person. She smiled as she walked through the mall, and even seemed to bounce. Then, from a distance, he saw Ellie walking with Joseph. They must have come from some social function: he was wearing a long-sleeved shirt tucked into dark slacks, and she a nice dress and high heels. Ted wondered if he should try to steer Gwen away.

He was about to speak when a male voice yelled "Dad!" It was Steven, followed by Eric, walking out of a game store. Ted raised his hand to greet them, and they walked toward him.

Gwen slowed down, then tried to walk away, but Ted grabbed her by the arm and pulled her forward. As the boys got close, their expressions changed.

"Well, Steven, Eric, aren't you going to say hello to your sister?"

The siblings stood looking at each other. Gwen was afraid to speak. She turned around and tried to leave again, but Ted stopped her. "Whoa… You're not running away—are you, Gwen?"

She turned to face her brothers—apologies and explanations scrolling across her face. "Hi," she said awkwardly.

"Hi," Eric said. "Jesus Christ, what'd you do to your hair?!"

Ted and Steven laughed, surprised and relieved. Gwen blushed. "Oh, I just wanted to see what it would be like to have short hair."

"So, you like it?" Eric made a face.

"Yeah...yeah, I do." Gwen turned to look at herself in a store window.

"Gwen...?"

She froze at the sound of her mother's voice. Turning slowly, she faced Ellie.

"Hi, Mom."

At one time, it had been hard to tell daughter from mother: the two dressed, talked, and behaved alike. Now they gazed at each other like strangers.

"Where have you been, Gwen? I've been worried about you."

"Yeah, I know. I'm sorry." She tensed up.

"Well, I'm glad your dad found you...and now *we* have. Your room is just as you left it, sweetheart: your clothes, shoes, jewelry—even your pictures. Everything is still there, waiting for you to come back. We can take you home with us—right, Joseph?"

"Right, of course," he replied, recovering quickly from his surprise. "We just came back from a wedding and stopped here because Steve and Eric wanted to look at some games. But we can go home right after they're done."

"No," Gwen said.

"What did you say, honey? 'No'?"

"I mean I don't want to go home with you, Mom. I have a home."

"You don't mean with your father?" Ellie asked, looking at Ted. "What kind of home can he give you, Gwen?"

"A nice home. I'm happy there."

"Well, you don't seem happy. And look at what you're wearing: a green blouse with baggy sleeves, a white belt, and faded brown pants. You look like you just came from a thrift shop."

"Actually—," Ted started to say.

"Mom, these *are* from a thrift shop. The one in Kaimukī. I chose them, and Dad bought them for me."

"Well, your clothes at home are much nicer. And you have decent shoes there too, not ugly slippers someone threw away."

"I don't want…" Gwen started to tremble.

Ellie moved closer and put her hand on Gwen's forearm. "Once you're home for a few days, it will be like you never left. We'll share clothes and makeup like we used to!" Ellie said with a little laugh. "You'll be your old self again."

"I don't want that! Don't you understand?!" Tears filled her eyes. "I don't want to be the old Gwen. That Gwen is *dead*. This," she said, striking her chest, "is the *new* Gwen."

The smile left Ellie's face, and she let go of Gwen's arm. "You can't want to stay with your dad. He can't help you, Gwen. Eventually, he will let you down, just as he's let me and everyone else down. One day that will happen to you too." Turning to Joseph, she said, "We should go home." They started to walk away.

Eric and Steven stood still, confused about what to do.

"Come, boys," Ellie said over her shoulder. "Boys, we are *leaving*."

"Fuck!" Eric said. "Goddamn stupid shit!" He turned and followed his mother.

"Sorry, Dad. See you, Gwen." Waving, Steven hurried to catch up.

Gwen wiped her face with the sleeve of her blouse. "You OK?" Ted asked. She nodded. He put his hand on her elbow and started to walk slowly. "Let's go find your glasses."

Gwen tried on a pair with light-pink frames.

"Are you sure you want that grapefruit color for your glasses?"

"Sure, why not? How do I look?"

"OK, I guess. Hides your pretty eyes."

"Well, maybe that's not a bad thing," she said, smiling.

"Can you see all right?"

"Not really. Everything is blurry. "

"Well, those are *reading* glasses, Gwen." They laughed, Gwen put the glasses back, and the bounce returned to her step.

"Hungry? Want to get something to eat?"

"Sure, how about some Korean food?" They went to a small shop nearby, ordered, and sat at a table.

"Dad, who was that guy Mom was with?"

"His name is Joseph. He's a friend of hers from church."

"You met him before?"

Ted's face tightened. "Yeah."

"And? Were they having an affair or something?"

"No-no, nothing like that…I came home from my security job one day, and he and your mom were sitting on the couch. Ellie confronted me."

"Confronted you? About what?"

"About…," Ted said, his face flushing, "my membership in an adult website." His voice trailed off.

Gwen's eyes widened. "You belong to an adult site?"

"*Belonged.* By the time Ellie discovered it, I'd cancelled my membership, but she didn't know that. When she confronted me, things got out of control so fast I didn't explain."

"You mean you got mad?"

"Yeah, I got mad, very mad."

"Why did you do that, Dad—join, I mean?"

"You wouldn't understand."

"Try me. A lot has happened to me since I left home that you don't know about, Dad."

"Even if that's true, I'd rather not tell you. There are some things kids should not know about their parents."

"I may not know much about parents, but I know plenty about men— believe me. Tell me, Dad. I want to know."

Ted began hesitantly.

"When we lived in Wahiawā and I was working part-time for the church, one of the elders attacked your mom. She had been flirting with him, and he took it the wrong way when she asked him to come over to the house. I wanted to beat the guy up, but she begged me not to do anything."

"I remember hearing about this. Mom told me."

"She already had an affair—about five years before you were born—"

"She did?"

"Yeah, she did. You may know a lot about men, but you don't know about women, do you? When the elder attacked her, I just couldn't take it. Everything came back—jealousy, rage, humiliation. Plus that, I was fired from the church, thanks to this guy. He set me up, and I left, disgraced. I had to scramble to find other part-time work. That's why I've had so many different jobs, Gwen. When you don't have experience, you have to settle for what you can get, and a lot of these jobs are short term. Or sometimes the boss's friend or nephew or whoever loses his job, and you're replaced by the guy. And you don't always get two weeks' notice.

"One night I was desperate to feel good any way I could. I searched for pornography on the computer and went to the first site that came up. And then I started looking at more sites. It was the only thing that could make me stop hurting. Do you know what that's like, Gwen? It's like being so hungry that you eat garbage. And of course, I was so mad at your mom that I didn't want to have anything to do with her. Porn was my revenge on her for all she'd done to me—and my revenge on the church too. As more things became available on the Internet, I followed like a dog eating scraps falling off a garbage truck. I couldn't stop, and it felt so good: pleasure without any penalty. I was doing things that I used to find rotten and disgusting when other men did them. Finally, it got me in trouble at the base."

"Oh no, did you get suspended?"

"No, but the base commander ordered me into counseling with a doctor, a Hawaiian woman—Charlene Ho'okano. We finished the sessions a couple months ago, but I still see her every few weeks as a private client."

"So are you cured?"

"Nope. I thought I could control myself, but then I had a relapse."

"You had a relapse? What happened?"

"I stopped at an Internet café and tried to watch a video. When I told the doctor, she said she'd have to put that in her report."

"Oh no!"

"Yeah, stupid guys like me need to be burned more than once to learn our lesson."

"Stupid or stubborn?"

"Stupid, stubborn—same smell."

"Dad, that day you found me, I had gotten a dose from a dealer I knew. I had no money to buy it, and I was desperate. I'd been living on the street for almost a week. He said he would give it to me, but I'd have to do something in return: make a movie—a short one. I'd done plenty of things to maintain my habit, and that was not a lot worse. I stole from people, betrayed friends, hustled guys, pretending to like them and then talking them out of their money. Sometimes the 'liking' got pretty intimate. One guy I knew really loved me, but he was an addict too. I started stealing from him, and he beat me up.

"I did it, Dad—made the movie. Afterward, I walked around in a daze. I had five dollars on me—all my money—and I stopped at a mini mart to buy some gum and get change. I saw they had a public phone, so I called Grandma—"

"Grandma?!"

"I was hoping she was still in the phone book, and she was. I made like everything was fine but I had to contact you for some legal reason. She gave me your number, but it was so hard to remember. I had to ask her to repeat it three times. She asked me if I was all right, and I lied. I said I would come by and visit her sometime. And then I called you. I was hoping you would pick up. I know you don't answer most of the time."

Ted shook his head, then leaned forward and closed his eyes, pressing his fingertips hard against the eyelids. He remembered reading in college a play about a king who had gouged out his eyes when he learned he was the source of the plagues in his country. Ted thought the playwright had exaggerated the man's agony, but suddenly the king's motivation became clear. For decades Ted had tried to lead his life by the book, but things had turned out all wrong—not only for himself but also for his family.

The sins of the father shall be visited upon the children. The Biblical verse bled into his conscience: Gwen's desperate existence was tied to his sordid Internet life. He put his hands down on the table.

"Gwen honey, I make this promise to you: as long as I am alive, you will never have to do that again."

"Mom was wrong—wasn't she, Dad? You won't let me down."

Ted could only shake his head.

"The old Gwen is dead. I killed her. That was one reason I wanted to cut my hair: I didn't want anyone recognizing the...the woman...in the movie as me." She looked into her father's eyes as if asking to be forgiven.

Ted stared at the girl who had survived her father's mistakes, her mother's, and her own. Finally he said, "I think we have to get the Camry back to Les. Ready to go?"

"Ready, willing, and able," Gwen said as she jumped to her feet.

i for impostor

"Gwen, Les and his mother want us to have dinner with them. Would you like to do that?"

"Sure! Should I make something?"

"Can you cook?"

"Well, I can make rice. I can boil eggs, make toast…"

"Let's leave the cooking to them, OK? We can bring dessert—a pie or something."

Gwen sat at the dining table and looked out the large picture window. In the distance was Diamond Head to the left, the Pacific in the middle, and Waikīkī to the right, so highly developed that the buildings nearly obliterated the ocean. Kaimuki's low commercial buildings and homes filled most of her view. She felt lucky to be removed from the noisy, busy areas of the city, to live in the Sierra Drive neighborhood. *Neighborhood, my neighborhood*—she savored the words.

"So dear, how do you like living with your father?" Mrs. Ogata had a sweet voice and spoke slowly, in perfect English, though she sometimes used pidgin when she addressed her son.

"It's OK," Gwen said. "He's a good cook." She smiled.

"What does he cook?"

"Oh, peanut-butter sandwiches, spam sandwiches, musubi, saimin, spaghetti sometimes..."

"Where do you sleep? The downstairs has only one bedroom."

"I sleep on the floor in the living room. Dad lets me use his folding mattress."

"Ah, I see...Lester, next weekend let's clean out my sewing room. Gwen can use that for a bedroom."

"Oh no," Ted said, "that's not necessary. We don't want to impose. Please."

"No imposition! I used to sew in there. It has my sewing machine and fabrics and patterns. Plus other things I made: embroidery, arts and crafts. But I don't sew anymore. Gwen can use the room."

"Don't you want to keep your fabrics and things?" Gwen asked.

"Some of those things can stay in there. I don't think they'll get in your way. I can donate the rest to the community center. It's no trouble at all. You're a young girl. You need your privacy."

Les listened without comment, wondering how Gwen's presence would affect him and his mother. No longer could he fall asleep in front of the TV, drooling onto his T-shirt, fart without embarrassment, or walk around the house wearing only his boxer shorts.

"Mrs. Ogata, that is awfully kind of you, but are you sure you and Les don't mind?"

Les started to answer. "Um, I—"

"No, of course we don't mind! It will be nice to have Gwen up here. Lester is a good boy, but it would be nice to have another female around." She smiled sweetly.

Gwen's mind raced as she imagined living upstairs with the Ogatas.

"But Gwen can't pay rent. She doesn't have a job," Ted said.

"Yet! I'm going to look for one, Dad."

"Oh, we'll work something out. Perhaps she can help cook and clean, do grocery shopping and other things."

Hmm, maybe won't be so bad, Les thought.

"Well, I don't really know how to cook, but I can clean!"

"I'll teach you, my dear. And I have cookbooks in the kitchen." Looking Gwen over, she said, "What size are you, dear? You're a skinny young thing. Size six?"

Gwen nodded.

"I have some old clothes stored away. From when I was young and pretty." She laughed. "Maybe you can fit them, dear."

Gwen tried to smile, but the thought of wearing Mrs. Ogata's decades-old clothes mortified her. She looked at her dad for help.

"That is very kind of you, Mrs. Ogata. Gwen doesn't need a large wardrobe. Her life is very simple these days, so a few things might be all she needs."

Gwen relaxed.

"All right. Lester, next weekend let's clean out the sewing room and get some of my things out of storage. Maybe we can even paint the room. What is your favorite color, dear?"

"I like yellow—sunflower yellow."

"OK, we'll try to find that color for you."

"I can do the painting," Ted said.

"Wonderful; thank you, Ted." Mrs. Ogata smiled, pleased with her plans. Ted, Gwen, and Les sat in silence, their minds reeling as they tried to anticipate the coming changes to their lives.

Ted and Gwen sat near the front of the stage. He had gotten off his security job at three, and they had had to race to the concert hall for the four o'clock performance.

He glanced at her. She was wearing one of Mrs. Ogata's pretty silk dresses: a light-blue Alfred Shaheen dress with long sleeves and a fabric belt. It turned out that Mrs. Ogata had been quite a dresser in her young days, and she had many clothes that lit up Gwen's eyes. *Those shoes don't match, though,* Ted thought. *We should get another pair. Maybe we'll go to the discount store next time.*

A slender Asian man carrying a violin walked onto the stage, and everyone applauded as he took his seat. Then the conductor, an older Caucasian man, appeared, again to applause. The conductor shook the hand of the Asian man first and then the hand of the woman violinist seated next to him. Ted watched with fascination. When he was young, he had tried to play the violin. A cousin had had an old one that he'd discarded when he got a better one, and Ted had tried to learn how to play. He knew how hard it was, and as a teenager, he was envious of those classmates who had gotten into the high school band. They often seemed to be the smarter, more popular kids.

After the first piece—a modern work that left Ted wondering why Mrs. Ogata would buy season tickets to hear such music—some of the orchestra members moved their chairs, and two men rolled a large black block onto the stage. They set it down on the floor and unfolded it, and it became a platform. Other men set up a microphone and small footrest on the platform. Then the conductor walked offstage, and the master musician came out: a middle-aged Japanese woman wearing a white kimono and carrying a shiny black shamisen. The conductor returned. When the woman turned to face the symphony orchestra, Ted's gaze lingered on the elegant crane pattern on her dark-blue obi.

As the orchestra performed the woman's composition—*I for Impostor, Concerto for Shamisen and Orchestra*—Ted saw that the conductor moved vigorously, striking the air with his baton, while staring at the musicians as if demanding them to fill the concert hall with sound. It occurred to him that the conductor, orchestra, and master musician were enacting a series of events—some sad, some dramatic, some peaceful—and these travelled down a long, twisting path.

Gwen watched intently as well, charmed by the woman. Despite the formality of the music, the woman smiled girlishly, obviously enjoying the performance of her composition.

During the intermission, Ted read the program.

This concerto looks at the impostor as a resident of the floating world of impermanence, illusion, and ambiguity. Are we all not concealing a secret self that comes and goes with our circumstances? Sometimes we find ourselves in a state of excitement, other times in a situation of great risk. If we are able to practice detachment, we can escape the floating world. But how many of us are able to do that? We continue, floating in the floating world.

Ted had no idea how what he had heard matched the woman's description, but her words deepened his appreciation of the effort. *The floating world*...he'd have to look that up sometime.

"How did you like the concert, Gwen?" Mrs. Ogata asked.

"It was cool!" Gwen said.

"So you liked it?"

"Yes, the master musician was very cool. She wore a beautiful white kimono and played the shamisen like a rock star!"

"Ah, well I'm glad you and your dad decided to use those tickets. Did you like it too, Ted?"

"Yeah, it was good—a real education in music. I'm glad we had a chance to go. Thank you, Mrs. Ogata. I haven't been in the concert hall since I was in high school, I think. We had to go for a class excursion."

"Me too!" Gwen said. "I haven't been there in ages."

"Lester used to come with me, but he would fall asleep, and I got tired of buying a ticket for someone who was always sleeping. I started going with my sister, but she couldn't make it this time."

"Maybe that's not his kind of music," Ted responded.

"Oh, but he was in the band in high school."

Ted looked at Les. "For real, Les? You was in band?"

"Eh, no talk so loud! People goin' hear you. Ruin my reputation." Les winked.

"What you wen play?"

"Try guess!"

"Um, the clarinet? The drums?"

"The bass!" Gwen said.

"No, da tuba."

"*Tuba*?! For real, Les? Not!"

"Really, das true—yeah, Mom?"

"Yes, Lester played the tuba. He was very good too! My husband and I were so proud of him. When the band marched at football games, we always took pictures."

"Wow, you marched too?!"

"Eh, I wasn't always fat, you know!"

"You not fat. You just have big clothes!" Ted laughed at his joke, slapping his knee.

Annoyed and embarrassed, Les blushed. Mrs. Ogata and Gwen tittered.

"Eh, jus' wait," Les said. "I show you. I goin' exercise *every* day. I goin' make *you* look fat!"

"OK, you got one deal. I tell you what: you lose weight, I take you Turtle Bay. We go try the buffet."

Les grinned at the offer.

"I'll exercise with you!" Gwen volunteered.

"You shuah?"

"Yeah, of course. Maybe we can start here: walk around the block."

"Yeah, start small," Ted said. "Gimme time to save my money."

"You got one deal, braddah," Les said, giving Ted a high five.

Mrs. Ogata beamed. "He'll do it. Lester can do it, I know."

It was seven a.m. when they left the house. Les wore a clean white T-shirt, black shorts, and a pair of old running shoes. Gwen put her hair in pigtails that stuck out behind her ears. She wore a white shirt and faded red shorts that Ted had found at a thrift shop and, instead of shoes, a pair of rubber slippers. The air was moist with the night's respiration, and a blue-gray haze hung over the houses and buildings in the distance. Gwen breathed in deeply, happy to be up and about at this hour. They would start Les's exercise regime today, walking once around the block.

"Should take mebbe twenny minutes," Les said. "We go slow. First time 'cause."

"Sure," Gwen responded, smiling.

"Eh, what dat on your shirt?"

"This?" Gwen said, grabbing the pocket. "I think that's a patch for the school. This is a school uniform my dad found."

"Ah...'CDL'? Mainland school dat?"

"Yeah, must be. Can't think of any local school with those initials."

Les walked ahead on the narrow path that people used for a sidewalk in this part of Sierra Drive. Gwen looked at the homes and yards, wondering about the owners. In one yard, she saw spindly white and purple orchids and was amazed at how tall and straight they could grow. There must have been at least fifty plants in the unweeded yard. She guessed that whoever had first planted them had long given up on trying to cultivate them. It was a wild garden, pretty and unsightly at the same time. *If only someone spent a little more time.* Her dad was good with plants, tending the trees in the Ogatas' yard as if they were members of the family. She thought of him muttering to himself as he worked in the yard.

"Eh, no fall behind," Les said.

"Oh, sorry." Les's steps were midsized and deliberate, Gwen's small and slow. The uneven path was new to her, and it dipped and rose unpredictably. People had graded the lots for their homes, but most had not touched the narrow edge next to the street. It remained rough and ragged.

Gwen and Les turned a corner. She peered at a house with a red-clay driveway and a single palm tree. The windows were closed, white curtains drawn across them. Dirt had stained the lower part of the house where it met the yard. The place seemed vacant.

She wondered if she'd ever have her own home. Her father didn't buy the Kāneʻohe house until he was in his fifties. The family had been poor for most of her life, living in rented homes, termite eaten and falling apart. Her thoughts wandered to the run-down apartment building she'd been living in shortly before her father found her.

"Awful place," she muttered to herself.

Les turned around. "You said someting?"

"I was thinking about where I was living before Dad found me at Kawānanakoa."

"Yeah?"

"Yeah, it was an old three-story apartment building in the area next to Kapiʻolani Boulevard, across from the cemetery."

"Oh yeah, I know da area."

"One night I was walking down the stairs, and I came across a guy slapping his girlfriend around..." Les waited as Gwen found her words. "I didn't like her. But still, I could have helped her: tried to stop him or call for help. But I didn't do anything...I ran away...I'm not a good person."

"Eh, no talk like dat. You good."

Gwen looked Les in the eyes and said, "No, I'm not, Les. You don't know what I've done. I'm not good. I used to hustle men for their money!"

He smiled as if he hadn't heard her. "Eh, I say you good—you good. No argue. You nevah help dat girl, but one big guy hitting her—how you goin' stop dat? You try stop him, he beat you up too, den what? You both go hospital."

"But I could have gotten help. I didn't do anything."

"You see her again?"

"Yeah, she had a black eye and spots on her arms. Looked like cigarette burns."

"Den what happened?"

"I ran away from my boyfriend soon after that and started living on the street. I was glad to get away from him and that awful place. A mom and her two kids were living in a two-bedroom apartment next door. The mom, Verna, beat the kids every night. We could hear them crying and running from room to room, trying to get away from her. My boyfriend called the wall between us the Wall of Hell. Have you ever heard the sound of a kid running, smashing into things, while his mom is scream-ing? It's the worst sound in the world..."

Les shook his head sadly. "Can imagine."

"I tried to hurt myself, you know."

"No, I nevah know."

"Yeah, a couple years ago. At first with needles, safety pins—poking my-self, then dragging them over my skin. Then I got some razor blades..."

"Why you do that for?"

"Not sure you would understand. When you hurt but don't know why—or can't say why—you have to do something. Know what I mean?"

"Guess so. But why nevah watch TV, call somebody, go beach...Your dad know?"

"Eventually, Mom and Dad found out and took me to the hospital. I shared a room with a girl my age, Carmella. She was very pretty."

"You pretty too."

"Maybe, but not like her. She had long, shiny brown hair and blue eyes. Her bangs were cut straight across her forehead, making her blue eyes stand out. When Dad and Mom came to see me in the hospital, they were really worried. Mom talked to me sweetly, trying to comfort me. After they left, the girl told me her mom had never talked to her that way. Her mom had always been mean, cold and abusive. She cried while she said that. She had tried to hurt herself too."

"Someday, you wait. Someday you get your chance stand up for somebody. Den you prove yourself. You no believe in you, but I do."

Tears started to fall from Gwen's eyes, and Les stood by helplessly. "Eh, no cry now! People goin' tink my fault!"

Gwen choked on a sob and let out a laugh. "OK," she said. They continued their walk. "Les, how come you never got married? You seem like such a nice guy."

He blushed. "I had one girlfriend at McKinley. Evelyn her name. We went KCC after graduate, for get associate degree. But she like go UH, and I nevah like. 'Enough awready,' I tol' her. She wen go UH, meet somebody. Dey got married, have big house in 'Āina Haina. Me—I stay home, work at da base. I sad nevah wen work out, but whachu can do, uh? Sometime one frien' or relative try introduce me to somebody, but I too shy. Or da girl fat or ugly or boring.

"Now just trying take care Mom. She old, but our family—we live long time: eighties, nineties. She still get lots time left, and she sharp, you know. She do da kine Sudoku puzzle every night! Ho, I cannot do even one!" Les laughed at himself, and Gwen laughed with him.

When they got back to the house, they found Mrs. Ogata had made a simple breakfast for them: coffee, scrambled eggs, and toast.

"So, dear, how was your walk?"

"It was nice."

"Lester didn't walk too fast for you?"

"Nope, not at all."

"Lester can walk fast—when he wants to." Les frowned. "Or when he smells something to eat." His frown grew deeper.

They sat quietly for several minutes, the tinging of silverware and plates the only sounds.

"Many years ago," Mrs. Ogata said, breaking the silence, "when I was a teenager and my family was living on Kaua'i, my parents had a friend. I think he had once worked for my father. This young man had gone off to the war in Korea and come back...well, different. He didn't smile and couldn't carry on a conversation. Every night, he would walk around the neighborhood and surrounding area wearing his dress uniform. It was summertime, and my mother suggested I walk with him to keep him company. I was just a child—sixteen years old—and he a mature man who had gone to war. We didn't speak, but three or four times a week, I would walk with him. It was awkward at first because I didn't know what to say and kept trying to make conversation. After a week, I became quiet too.

"We would walk for over an hour in the dark. At that time, the streets weren't lit well, and in spots the only light came from the moon and people's houses. I never felt afraid, though, because he was with me, and I trusted him. After a month or so, my parents told me he was moving here, to Oʻahu. He came by one afternoon and brought a present for me: a small Japanese doll in a glass case."

"Dat da one in your bedroom?" Mrs. Ogata nodded. "Pretty dat."

"Yes, it is. Gwen, the doll is of a girl maybe twelve. She has shoulder-length hair and a round face. Her pink mouth is very delicate, like a rosebud. She wears a green kimono with a small flower pattern, and carries a blue lantern in one hand. Her other hand is raised toward her face."

"Sounds gorgeous," Gwen said.

"You evah see da guy again?"

"No, never." Mrs. Ogata's eyes grew moist. "When he told me he was leaving, I was so sad that I cried—without really understanding why. That was the first time I had adult feelings I didn't understand—strong feelings and no words. Later I realized that that was how he was feeling all the time. It was harder for him, of course. He'd seen and done too much—too much that was bad—for his heart and mind to express."

"But by walking—," Gwen started.

"By walking with him, I was standing with him." Mrs. Ogata smiled. "My presence said all the things I couldn't say."

prayers

ℵ

It was a cool Tuesday evening. That morning, Ted and Les had had training for their recertification as mechanics. They'd decided to celebrate their early quitting time by eating at a place in Chinatown. They ordered the Italian restaurant's homemade lasagna and hot grilled sandwiches, and Gwen got a tuna salad with warm slices of ciabatta bread.

When they left, it was just after seven o'clock, and a full moon lit the clouds. Gwen slipped her hands inside the pockets of her light jacket.

Walking ahead in quick steps, Les hurried to the public parking garage three blocks way. Ted and Gwen took their time. When a person would approach from the opposite direction, they would walk single file on the narrow sidewalk. A slender Chinese man stepped out of a shop, turned around, and drew two wide, wooden doors together, then slipped a padlock on them. A cream-colored pug dog waited at his heels. A haole man stationed on the sidewalk opened the door to a soup kitchen, and several people left, smiling. He kept the door open as the next ones in line stepped forward and went in; then he closed it as the rest waited their turn.

Coming to a traffic light, Gwen saw a thin young man standing next to a woman with short black hair and tattooed arms. He was wearing boots, tight jeans, and a dark, long-sleeved shirt with the cuffs rolled up. He had a chunky chain around his neck and a wide leather band on his wrist. He and the woman waited on the other side of the street for the light to change.

Gwen tried to look away, hoping the young man wouldn't notice her. The light changed, and Ted stepped into the street.

"Hey ya, Gwen!" the young man said as he passed her. Gwen looked at him but didn't respond. She continued walking.

"Who was that?" Ted asked.

"No one."

"A no one who knows your name?"

"Forget it, Dad."

"Someone you used to know?" Ted stopped and looked at Gwen. "The guy who made the movie?" Gwen didn't respond. Ted cupped her face in his hands. "The guy who made the movie?" he repeated, his voice harsh. She didn't reply. Her cheeks became hot, and tears filled her eyes.

Ted started walking in the direction they'd come from.

"*Dad! Dad!*" Gwen yelled, trying to keep up as he strode after the young man.

On reaching the couple, Ted put his hand on the man's shoulder and spun him around.

"*What the fuck?!*" Ted could smell his foul breath and see his rotting teeth.

"You know my daughter?!" Ted demanded.

"I don't know anyone related to you, you fucking monkey." Ted put his hand on the man's shoulder again, swiftly turned him around, and twisted his arm around his back. The two men were about the same height, but Ted was much heavier. Ted said into his ear, "I ever see you again, I'm going to kill you. You got that, you scum?"

The man struggled and, raising his foot, stomped on Ted's bare instep with his boot heel. The pain shot through Ted, and he jerked back. Breathing hard, he pushed the young man forward, slammed him into a wall, and threw him on the ground.

The young man turned to look up at Ted, saliva falling from his mouth. He reached into his back pocket and drew out a penknife. Gwen, the tattooed woman, and some bystanders watched, unable to intervene.

Seeing Gwen, Les yelled, *"Gwen! You coming or what?!"*

As if coming out of a trance, the small crowd broke up, and Ted turned to see Les walking toward them. The woman helped the young man up. Ted turned again to see them disappearing down the sidewalk.

Les watched as Ted took deep breaths and, grimacing, straighten his back. "Eh, you wen run up Tant'lus or someting?"

As they took the freeway to Kaimukī, Gwen sat in the back of the Camry. The hundreds of city lights outshone the few stars. She lay down on the seat, bringing up her knees. Quietly, so that Les and her father wouldn't hear her, she cried.

𝓧

Les drove Gwen to Kaimukī Library, the district branch, so that she could use one of the public computers. Right inside the door was a stand with brochures and pamphlets. She pulled one out and read: "The mission of the Hawaii State Public Library System is to provide Hawaii's residents, in all walks of life, and at each stage of their lives, with access to education, information, programs and services, and to teach and nurture the love of reading and the habit of life-long learning."

"Do I need a library card to use the computers?" Gwen asked the librarian sitting at the front of the computer section.

"Yes, you do."

"I...don't have one."

"I have!" Les volunteered. "Here, use mines."

The librarian narrowed her eyes at them, but took Les's card, murmuring to herself.

"Thank you, Les," Gwen said, smiling.

"Shuah. I goin' browse da stacks. Be back in fifteen, twenny minutes, 'kay?"

She nodded, then sat down at a computer, feeling shy and self-conscious. She opened her email and composed a message to herself, typing what she remembered of the night before.

My dream. I was in a long, narrow park with lots of trees. I realized the friend I was with was gone. To look for her, I got on a moped and rode on the dirt path that led to the end of the park. The moped hardly made any noise. Then I rode back to the entrance. Along the way, I saw shelters or cabins. These were open, so I could see inside. Each had a little kitchen and some supplies. One had a large bathroom. Another had stairs that led to a loft. Suddenly I sensed a man behind me. But I didn't panic. I followed the dirt path out of the park. I didn't struggle, scream, run like in other dreams. I don't know why. Maybe something has changed?

Putting her hands down, Gwen looked at the computer screen and read over her words. A few seats down, a Filipino boy was speaking to an older man, probably his father, in a mixture of English and their own language. The boy kept pointing to the computer screen and asking his father if he understood. The older man nodded, grunted, occasionally getting flustered and cursing softly. Gwen thought about her father, who never swore.

Then she thought of Charlene Hoʻokano. She typed the doctor's name in the search field, and three pages of results appeared. She scanned the entries, her eyes resting on an interview. She clicked on the link and was taken to the website of the Carlton Theological Seminary. The doctor's interview, said the first paragraph, was one of a series done with women psychologists who had earned doctorates at Carlton.

Dr. Hookano was born into a Hawaiian-Portuguese family that has lived for six generations on the Big Island, the largest of the fiftieth state's main islands. After earning her doctorate at the Pasadena campus in 1986, Dr. Hookano returned home to begin private practice. She now heads the employee assistance program at a military installation and maintains a private practice on the main island of Oahu.

CTS: Can you tell us why you decided to come here to obtain your doctorate?

CH: I came from a large family of five girls and one boy. I was the oldest and was about to start at the University of Hawaii when tragedy struck. My younger sister, sixteen years old, was murdered. We eventually learned that she had struggled with a man attempting to rape her, and he flew into a rage and strangled her. He threw her body into a large crater, and it was only after he confessed a week later that we were able to find her. My mother had a nervous breakdown, and my father went into a deep silence broken by violent outbursts. I withdrew from UH to take care of Mom and look after my siblings. For a year, I tried to keep the family together.

In searching for strength and understanding at this time, I was counseled by a pastor who told me about the seminary. I went to the library to read about it, and then I sent away for information. I realized that Carlton could show me how to strengthen my faith, care for my family, and serve my community. I applied and was fortunate enough to obtain a scholarship. Once I arrived at the school, I got a part-time job and my family helped me from time to time with small loans.

The interview continued for two more pages. When Les returned, Gwen asked for his help in printing it out.

That evening, she read the interview to her father when he joined her and the Ogatas for dinner. Mrs. Ogata and Les listened quietly. Gwen looked at her father and saw that his eyes were impassive but his body was tense. He clasped his hands, resting them under his chin, and sat rigidly. She decided to stop reading after the first page. While she and the Ogatas ate, her father sat in silence. Only as they were finishing did he start to eat.

While Gwen washed the dishes, her father wiped them. "Dad, why did you get so quiet when I read the interview?"

"You wouldn't understand, Gwen."

"When haven't I understood what you've told me, huh? When?" She gripped the edge of the sink.

"At the end of the last session I had with Charlene, I felt like she was judging me, and I got angry and…said she was a pampered middle-class liberal who'd never suffered."

"What did she say?"

"She just looked at me and said that she meant her statements to be fair and objective, not critical. Then she said that I was free to find another doctor if she wasn't helping me."

"And…?"

"I haven't gone back. That's all I want to say, Gwen. This topic is closed." Ted draped the dishcloth on the handle of the oven and left.

Gwen listened to the front door open and close. *What a goddamn stupid guy,* she thought as waves of frustration fell over her.

Ted called Charlene's office and made an appointment for the end of the month. When he walked into her office, she turned to face him. She watched him sit before she spoke. "I'm surprised to see you, Ted. I got the impression that you wanted to find another doctor."

"Well, I did. Actually, I didn't want to see any doctor. But something has happened. My daughter was curious about you and found an interview with you—the one you did for the Carlton Theological Seminary."

"Yes, they did a series on female psychologists who got doctorates there."

"Yeah, Gwen read that to me. Can I ask you a couple questions?"

"Of course."

"First of all, Carlton respects the sacredness of marriage, but you didn't try to talk me out of leaving Ellie. Also, Carlton teaches that homosexuality is immoral, as the Bible says, but I remember—"

"Yes, that I said homosexuality falls within the normal range of human behavior."

"So how could you say those things, violating your beliefs and your training?"

"In my practice, I have counseled homosexuals and tried to reorient them. Usually, they resisted and ended up finding another doctor. About four years ago, I discovered that one of my nieces had a female partner. They got married in a state that allowed it, and three years ago my niece tried to have a baby using in vitro fertilization. After several attempts, she became pregnant, and now she and her spouse are the parents of a little boy. My sister—her mother—and I are close, so news of these things was always shared with me. When I went to visit my niece last summer, I found her happy and at peace with herself."

"But Carlton—"

"The seminary is developing a new attitude toward homosexuals. This is evident in its allowing campus clubs with homosexual members. Homosexuality itself is not condoned, but the groups are allowed to meet and have activities consonant with Carlton's theology and philosophy."

"Sounds like doubletalk to me."

"Well, you are not alone. Criticism has been leveled at Carlton, but thus far the school has not withdrawn its permission."

"And it's liberalized its attitudes toward marriage too?"

"In keeping with tradition, Carlton teaches that marriage reflects the covenant between man and God. When there is violence, however, the marriage cannot continue. In your case, there were many acts of adultery—"

"But for a long time—"

"Your heavy involvement in adult and porn sites constitutes adultery, Ted. In addition, there is evidence that the injury you and your wife did to your marriage resulted in harm to your children: your daughter's drug addiction and near death; your sons' involvement in violent, pornographic games. And of course, there were indirect results, such as the federal investigation. For those reasons, I felt it was legitimate to support a decision for you and your wife to separate."

"So I am as guilty as Ellie?"

"If you want to use those terms, we can say that each of you violated the marriage covenant in numerous ways numerous times. Each of you is to be pitied for acting selfishly and destructively."

"But I tried to keep my family together."

"You ride a motorcycle, Ted. Let's use it as a metaphor for your life. The front wheel was moving fast, propelled by the back wheel. Until recently, that wheel got its momentum from an immoral source. You were seeking out deviant sexual experiences. Because the people in front of you could only see you moving toward them, you were able to conceal what you were really doing. It was only because your secret life became public that the back wheel stopped moving—the whole machine stopped. Isn't that true?"

Ted didn't reply.

"You concealed things not only so people wouldn't know what you were really doing but also so you could maintain your status in your family and workplace. It was a false authority that you exerted over the lives of others. Now you must reconstruct who you are." Charlene moved her chair closer to him and leaned forward. "This is my prayer for you, Ted: that you seek, find, and accept the help you need. Reach out, Ted, please. I promise it will not hurt you."

"I...I..." Unable to continue, Ted stood up and left.

returning

Les held open the glass door to the ramen shop. Seeing that all the tables were taken, he and Gwen sat at the long, U-shaped counter. Opening onto the kitchen, it allowed the wait help to serve everyone at the counter quickly and efficiently.

Gwen glanced at the couple across from her, then started watching them, curious. The woman was slender, blonde, and fair skinned and wore a black, high-necked dress. Her thick eyebrows were also blonde, and she wore no makeup. She had put her shoulder-length hair in a low ponytail that rested against her back.

The man was dark skinned, thinner than the woman, and wore a tan nylon jacket over a white shirt. His thick, wavy black hair was parted neatly on the side, and his eyeglasses had heavy, conservative frames. He seemed preoccupied

The woman was turned slightly toward the man, as if wanting to share his thoughts and feelings. A kind, patient look was on her face. He didn't look at her, didn't speak.

The woman then pulled the light-blue band off her ponytail, took the man's hand, and put the band around his wrist. It seemed an odd gesture and yet so intimate, as if she were telling him something in a language of gestures that only they understood. He pulled on the band a bit, looking at it, thinking. When their meal arrived, they ate in silence. Families and couples sat around them, talking, gesturing with their chopsticks.

Obviously the man and woman were a couple, but happy, unhappy, married, not? Gwen couldn't tell. *I guess this is how some couples are. They don't need to speak, smile, or even look at each other. But their love seems deep.* She noticed that when the man looked at the blue band and touched it, he seemed to soften, his mood to lose its somber, dark edge. Why was the woman so patient, willing to wait for his words, his thoughts, his attention? He had something of value, something he wasn't free to give—his heart perhaps? Commitment to her?

They left, not even speaking when they paid their tab—returning to, Gwen imagined, a life enfolded in privacy.

Later in her room, Gwen thought about her parents, wondering when they had stopped loving each other. An image of her father formed in her mind. He was shirtless and sitting in a dark room at a desk with a small lamp. In front of him, magazines were scattered. He was looking at several at the same time, and as he went from one to another, he smiled or sighed. There he was by himself in the dark, the only light shining on pictures of half-dressed or nude women. A poor, pathetic man, barely able to support his wife and three kids, but he had a hoard of pornography to make himself feel better, to combat his loneliness, shame, and despair.

Gwen felt anger and disgust. Then self-pity overwhelmed her as she remembered the times she and her mother had conspired against him, deceived and isolated him. Was she any better than her mother—any less toxic? Gwen had had multiple boyfriends several times, leading them on, lying to them, getting them to buy her things or do favors for her. Eventually, they found out about each other, got mad, and left. Every now and then, someone would come back and try to reenter her life. Her father never bothered to learn their names.

I am my mother's child. But I am also my father's. Dad's sense of honor and self-respect are not completely gone. He saved me and brought me here. Part of him is still good. There is at least one blessing in my inheritance!

✶

One morning, Gwen asked Ted if they could go back to the Kāneʻohe home. "I need to get some things," she said.

"What do you need? I can probably buy it for you cheap."

"No, Dad, that's not it. I want to get my old computer and maybe—I don't know—see if there's anything else from the house I want to bring here."

"OK, well, I don't have a key anymore, so we'll have to call and see if one of the boys will let us in." Ted picked up his cell phone and dialed the number. After several rings, Steven answered. "Steven, this is Dad. Your sister wants to come by and get her computer and maybe some other things. Your mom at work?"

"Yeah, Dad—she's at the church. What time are you thinking?"

"How about in an hour—ten thirty? Les and I have to get ready to leave for work around one, so we'll have to make it quick."

Gwen nodded to indicate her agreement.

Ted borrowed Les's car and got on H-1. Deciding to use an alternate route to Kāneʻohe, he got off at the exit by the YMCA and took Likelike Highway. Gwen thought about the time she'd tried to come home. She'd lingered outside the house, unable to decide if she should knock. She was feeling remorseful, wanting to be forgiven. But she was also high, and when she stood outside, the old resentments and regrets flooded her thoughts. She had stood there swaying like a pole and then decided to leave.

As her father parked the car, she started to tense up. "You coming?" he asked when she remained seated.

After several seconds, she said, "Yeah…I'm coming."

They opened the gate, walked to the door, and rang the bell. Steven answered, looking at Gwen and trying not to stare. "Hey, Dad…Gwen."

"Hi, son. OK if Gwen goes straight to her room? We don't have a lot of time."

"Yeah, of course." Gwen stepped out of her slippers and into the small foyer. The banister leading to the second floor still had the decorative leaf pattern her mother had put on it when they'd first moved in. Gwen ran her hand along it, surprised to find it intact. She walked up the stairs, breathing in the smells of the house, everything seeming familiar and strange at the same time.

When she got to her room, she stood awhile in the doorway, gazing at the furniture, closet, pictures on the walls. A few of her clothes were poking out of the closet, and her old shoes sat beneath them. She winced, noticing the high-heeled shoes and the fur-covered boots. She stepped in and walked to her desk. Long ago, the family had given her a large bulletin board as a birthday gift, and it hung above the desk, covered with pictures, mementoes of happy events, greeting cards, ribbons, and other things. So many memories clung to it that she looked away. She unplugged her computer, keyboard, and mouse and put them on the bed. She got some paper, pens and pencils, notebooks and folders out of the desk and put them beside the computer. She looked at the photographs carefully, wondering if she should take any.

Her gaze fell on a framed picture on her desk, a formal portrait taken at a photographer's studio. Looking very pretty in a white dress, her mother sat in front with Eric on her lap. On her left was Steven, and on her right Gwen. Behind Steven was Ted, wearing an aloha shirt, and next to him were his parents, Aaron and Kimiko. Aaron was shorter than Ted and had narrow shoulders. He looked at the camera with a stoic expression. Kimiko had curly salt-and-pepper hair, wore eyeglasses, and smiled. *Dad was handsome when he was young,* Gwen thought. *We all look nice—so wholesome and normal.* She picked up the picture and put it on top of the computer.

Then she walked to the closet and pushed the door aside, releasing the smells of hopes and disappointments past. She raised her hand tentatively, then touched a few things: a long muumuu she had worn when the family celebrated her high school graduation, a maroon-and-white athletic sweater a guy on the basketball team had given her, a white silk blouse Grandma and Grandpa had bought her when she turned sixteen. She crushed the sleeve in her hand, then let go with a start.

"Hey, Gwen. Need any help? Oh sorry, didn't mean to scare you," Ted said when he saw her startled face. He and Steven stood in the doorway.

"I want to take these things," she said, pointing to the bed.

"OK, good. Steven, let's find a couple boxes we can put Gwen's stuff in." They turned to leave.

Embarrassed by the intensity of her feelings, Gwen faced the closet again and started to cry. She rushed to the bathroom to get tissue to wipe her face, then looked at herself in the mirror to see how red her eyes were. She heard Ted and Steven coming up the stairs and rushed back to her room. They'd found three boxes, plus a couple of shopping bags.

"What about your clothes and shoes?" Steven asked.

"Um, a lot of the clothes are too big for me now...Tell Mom she can keep them or give them away."

"Gwen, don't you want *anything*?" Ted asked.

"I...Can you guys let me do this myself?"

"Sure, Gwen. Come on, Steven. Gwen, you yell when you're ready."

Ted and Steven walked back down the stairs and into the living room. Ted pushed aside a stack of old newspapers on the couch and sat down.

"So, how are things with your mom?"

"Oh, OK. She hardly spends any time here. Most of the time she's at

Joseph's house. He lives in one of those townhouses on Mokulele Drive—where the rich guys live."

"Are they serious?"

"Seems like it. Sometimes she jokes that they'll get married and let Eric and me keep the house."

Ted looked around the messy room and concluded that that would be a terrible idea. "Well, she would be a bigamist since we're still married."

"What's happening with that?"

"I'm taking it slow. Divorce is a huge thing—lots of things to consider."

"How about you and Gwen? Are you going to stay at...at...?"

"The Ogatas.' They've been very nice to us. At the beginning, I was going to help Les take care of the house and his mom. But she, Mrs. Ogata, suggested that Gwen move into a room upstairs. So Gwen is pretty much keeping her company, doing the housework and grocery shopping, learning to cook."

Steven rolled his eyes.

"Hey, your sister has hope. She made a mac-and-cheese dish the other night that was pretty good. How about you? What are you doing these days? Looking for a job, I hope."

"Yeah, I keep filling out applications, going to places and asking if they have work. I would like to do computer stuff, but there are so many people doing that. Maybe I'll start my own business." Steven smiled broadly. "Steven Koga: Digital Valet."

"What's a digital valet?"

"Kind of like a butler or assistant—maybe someone who keeps track of home things—"

"Home inventory—"

"Yeah, property, things in storage, things to sell..."

"Sounds like it might work. Any prospects yet?"

"Nothing yet. Maybe I could start with Grandma and Grandpa. They've been collecting things for fifty years!" Steven laughed, and Ted joined him.

"Dad, Eric and I no longer use your old laptop. We pooled our money from Grandma and Grandpa and got a notebook. Do you want the laptop back?"

Ted started to shake his head, then reconsidered. It had been tough trying to get along without his own computer. He'd had to find Internet cafés, use Les's when he could, try to do a few things on the one he had access to at work. He could use his cell phone, but it wasn't a smartphone, so its capabilities were limited. Sometimes he had to hand deliver documents or depend on the postal mail. He needed the laptop, but it had gotten him into trouble and could again. He decided to take it and see if he could set it up in the Ogatas' living room. Mrs. Ogata was amiable and kind, but she expected everyone around her to adhere to her moral standards. Under her watchful eye, Ted would be less likely to experience failure. Les's disapproval would be silent but demoralizing nonetheless and would hurt their professional relationship as well as personal one. And, of course, there were his good buddies: the Feds would be tracking him as soon as data started transmitting from his laptop's IP address.

"Dad...Dad!" Steven's voice interrupted his thoughts. "Do you want the laptop or not?"

"Oh sorry, Steven. Just thinking...Have you boys done anything to it since I last used it?"

"Well, Joseph looked at it. Actually, he looked at all the computers and checked them for viruses and malware. He said that the laptop seemed to be the most infected. He thinks that the malware could have transmitted personal information, so you should be careful, Dad. Someone might have your financial data and other stuff. We put your files—after nuking them for viruses—on a new flash drive and deleted them from the laptop."

"What about the apps?"

"Joseph reinstalled the operating system and deinstalled the browser. So you'll have to reinstall it. Eric and I didn't touch it after that."

"Sounds like a smart guy. How do you like him? Is he nice to you and Eric?"

"Oh, he's all right. But he's not like you, Dad."

"How so?"

"I don't know. He's just not like you." Steven smiled.

That's my boy, Ted thought, and smiled too. "Sure, I'll take the laptop."

"Yeah, you might need it for work."

"Well, no, not really. But I can watch videos on paragliding."

"Paragliding?"

"Yeah, I'm thinking of—"

"I'm ready!" Gwen yelled.

"OK, we're coming."

Gwen had used all the boxes and bags. Thinking Mrs. Ogata might be able to teach her how to take in her clothes, she had packed her pants, shorts, and tops in the largest box. She'd put her shoes and handbags in another box, and the keyboard, mouse, cables, and writing supplies in the last. One shopping bag held the framed picture, jewelry, and other small items, and another held the long muumuu and her undergarments.

"Got everything?"

"Yeah, I think so."

"What about this bulletin board?"

"No, it's too big and bulky, and all kinds of things are hanging on it."

"But it has all your cards, souvenirs…"

"I know. Let's leave it here, OK? Maybe Mom will want to look at it sometime."

"Yeah, she might get lonely…and want to look at it," Steven said.

Everyone became quiet. When Ted picked up the computer, Gwen realized her favorite blanket was on the bed, along with a pillow with a monogrammed case. She rolled the pillow in the blanket and put them on top of the computer.

"Hand me that shopping bag, Gwen." She handed her father the bag, and he strode out.

⚡

"Eh, your one dirty," Les said to Gwen at the dinner table. They'd just cleaned the car, and she'd missed some grease along the edge of her hand.

"What?"

"Your one dirty. You need for wash 'em." Les held up his hand and ran his finger along the edge.

"Why do you call it 'your one'?" Gwen asked.

"Whachu mean?" Les looked perplexed.

"Why don't you just say 'Yours is dirty'?"

"Whaz wrong with 'your one'? Everybody say dat."

"Lester," Mrs. Ogata interjected, "'your' is a pronoun and so is 'one.' English speakers usually don't combine pronouns the way you just did."

"Oh yeah. Pro noun."

"No, no. *Pronoun*—one word."

"Where da kine—emphasis?"

"The accent is on the first syllable."

"For real?"

"For real, Lester." Mrs. Ogata rolled her eyes.

"Mom was one AP English teacher at McKinley."

"AP English?" Gwen asked.

"Advanced Placement: da class wid all da brains."

"You could have been in that class, Lester, if you'd studied harder and didn't go out with your band friends so much."

"Was fun but. And was all group dates. We nevah got in trouble."

"For real?" Mrs. Ogata asked.

"For real, Mom." Les sounded sincere, but he looked sheepish.

Gwen went to the kitchen sink and washed her hand. Returning, she cleared her throat. "I'm thinking of getting a part-time job," she announced.

"Really, dear? Where?"

"I think I have two choices. Kaimukī Library has volunteer positions, and I saw a sign at Goodwill saying they are hiring people."

"That's an excellent idea, Gwen. Have you talked to your father about getting a job?"

"No. I want to do it myself, then surprise him," she replied, smiling.

Les opened his mouth.

"Well, dear, if you need a reference, you can put me down."

"Gee, thank you so much!"

"You need help with da job application, jus' let us know. We give you good recommendation."

Pleased and happy, Gwen beamed. *Someday,* she thought, *I will repay you two—somehow.*

the floating world

ℵ

Ted stood on the ridge above Makapuʻu Beach, double-checking his harness, lines, and risers. He'd bought the paraglider from someone on Craigslist: Martin Lee, an older Chinese man who lived in Waiʻanae. The year before, Lee made a jump, then was found unconscious by two hikers. They called 911, and he was airlifted off the side of the mountain and taken by ambulance to a hospital. Most of the injury to his spine and legs was corrected by surgery, but he hadn't been able to do any gliding after the accident. Ted had wanted to talk about the sport, but Lee was interested in other things. They'd talked for two hours, Lee describing his tours of duty as a paratrooper in the 82nd Airborne Division and Ted telling him about his service in the Air National Guard. Toward the end,

Ted got him to lower the price for the glider from $1000 to $800. It had been an expensive model, but the damage was serious. Thinking he could repair it, Ted spent a month patching and resewing the nylon and going over every inch of the lines to make sure they would hold. He'd had to withdraw the money from a retirement account, but felt the expense was worth it. For decades he'd longed to be back in the air.

Now he closed his eyes and felt the sunlight and cool mountain breeze on his face. Images from videos he'd watched came to mind: people gliding as beaches or mountain slopes passed beneath them. He had briefly considered taking a training course, but it was too expensive. With two dozen jumps in the Guard, he figured he could manage. Then he thought of Gwen, volunteering at the library and working among the stacks of books. Perhaps she'd open them one day and discover stories and ideas she'd never thought of. Maybe she would even go back to school. These thoughts pleased him, and he opened his eyes. He was hoping for a twenty-minute flight or longer, and the winds seemed to be cooperating. He walked to the edge and looked down.

Then he was gliding through the air.

The sharp narrow ridges were covered in green from the recent rains. The sky was clear, and the only sound Ted heard was the glider riding the wind. He felt a deep peace. He turned his body to look at the ocean. When he looked back, he realized he had changed the glider's direction and was moving swiftly toward the mountain face. He pulled on the lines and risers and glided safely away.

How easy it is to kill yourself, he thought. *That's why people do it, isn't it?* The old desire for a lasting, simple peace came back to him, and he imagined what would happen with other tugs on the lines and alternate shifts of his weight. How great to finally be free of the burden and pull of all those memories and failures—the shame and grief. It would solve so many things.

He imagined his body limp on the rocks, the glider a broken wing, and the lines spread around him like puppet strings. Then he saw the dead man raise his arms and reach out to him. Ted's heart raced, and he stopped breathing. The flesh on the face had contracted, hugging the skull. The mouth was dark, the teeth yellow. No life shone in the eyes, just a pitiless blackness.

Suddenly a draft of warm air found the glider, lifting Ted out of the embrace of the devil he knew.

acknowledgements

Bedeviled is a work of fiction, but it contains the truth of the lives of many people. I thank those friends and family who shared their stories with me. The women in my writing group—Connie Pan, Angela Nishimoto, and Mary Archer—read early drafts of portions of this book. Manuscript versions were read by Phyllis Young, Perle Besserman, and Shawna Yang Ryan. I thank them all for their kind words and encouragement.

Much of *Bedeviled* was written in late afternoons and early evenings at the Coffee Bean and Tea Leaf at the Pearl City Shopping Center. Other evenings were spent at the Barnes & Noble store at Ala Moana Center. I thank the Coffee Bean staff for making my times there especially pleasant and productive.

⅋ The Fish Catcher

Petronium Press, 1985
ISBN 978-0-9321360-8-4

Each poem cuts through to the deep center and then begins to resonate and echo there, like a pebble thrown right into the pool of my life. *James D. Houston*

⅋ Stray

El León Literary Arts and Mānoa Books, 2006
ISBN 978-0-9762983-8-0

Evocative, sensuous, plangent, the poems in Pat Matsueda's long-awaited book are charged with the phenomenal world. Line by line, phrase by phrase, these poems won't go away: when you close your eyes, they are there; when you open your eyes, they are still there. *Arthur Sze*

It is an immensely gratifying book, and I will treasure it as one of the best in my collection.
Gene Frumkin

Such wise, tender, and beautiful poems! *Molly Giles*

I'm reading *Stray*, one poem a day, and finding my first good opinion more than justified—it's the best book to come my way in a long time. *Michael Hannon*

⅋ Ms. Aligned: Women Writing About Men

Edited with Sheyene Foster Heller
Aligned Press, 2016
ISBN 978-1-3299707-7-9

The writings in *Ms. Aligned* are, in the original sense of the word, astonishing—yes, they surprise us, but they also stun, bewilder, and dismay. Whatever the best expectations for such a collection may be, this one lives up to them. And more important, it exceeds them.
Hayan Charara

The female perspectives presented here—male creations/female creators—dissect, prod, query, challenge, validate, negotiate, and, ultimately, emancipate the gender boundaries that we otherwise take for granted. The effect is a wonderful loosening of the physical world, of our selves.
Samrat Upadhyay

rature / Fiction / Hawaii

Bedeviled
A NOVELLA

"Complex, in moments dark and in others wonderfully hopeful, *Bedeviled* is, at its heart, about the struggle to forgive the self. When Ted Koga's addiction is outed and his career threatened, he tries to root out the evil in his life, not understanding just how deeply past betrayals, resentments, anger, and hurt can burrow, and how difficult it is to escape old patterns. *Bedeviled* asks essential questions: How do we process hurt? How do we forgive wrongdoing? And how do we heal, with—or without—the support of our families? Through her carefully crafted characters, Matsueda makes these philosophical questions powerfully real, and though she resists easy answers, her novella offers a sense of hope and vision."

KRISTIANA KAHAKAUWILA, AUTHOR OF THIS IS PARADISE: STORIES

"*Bedeviled* digs deeply into the emotional costs of addiction—sexual and substance—through the story of a family that self-destructs and then quietly stitches itself back together. With an empathetic eye, Matsueda explores addiction's roots in abuse and loneliness, and demonstrates how confronting pain—and making oneself vulnerable to love—can be a way to freedom. A dark, moving, and, ultimately, hopeful story."

SHAWNA YANG RYAN, AUTHOR OF GREEN ISLAND

"Resonant and true to place, Pat Matsueda's mesmerizing novella offers a glimpse into the unraveling of one man's life, along with a close look at a Hawai'i few outsiders know. Matsueda is a master wordsmith."

PHYLLIS GRAY YOUNG, AUTHOR OF SEA HOME

"*Bedeviled* is a beautiful metaphor, surprising, riveting, and honest. Within its pages, Internet porn and the floating world seem made for each other, and are grounded in the human heart. The prose is spare and searching; the overall effect is luminous."

ROBERT SHAPARD, COEDITOR OF FLASH FICTION INTERNATIONAL

Pat Matsueda is the author of *Stray*, coeditor with Sheyene Foster Heller of *Ms. Aligned*, and managing editor of *Mānoa: A Pacific Journal of International Writing*.

A PUBLICATION FROM

Mānoa Books manoafoundation.org

León Literary Arts elleonliteraryarts.org

ISBN 978-0-9799504-1-4

9 780979 950414

BEDEVILED

Bedeviled

a novella by Pat Matsueda

PAT MATSUEDA · MĀNOA BOOKS · EL LEÓN LITERARY ARTS